T0304964

THE NORTH SHORE

BEN TUFNELL

FLEET
2023

FLEET

First published in Great Britain in 2023 by Fleet

1 3 5 7 9 10 8 6 4 2

A CIP catalogue record for this book
is available from the British Library.

ISBN 978-0-349-72730-1

Typeset in Garamond by M Rules
Printed and bound in Great Britain by Clays Ltd, Elcograf S.p.A.

Papers used by Fleet are from well-managed forests
and other responsible sources.

MIX
Paper from
responsible sources
FSC® C104740

Fleet
An imprint of
Little, Brown Book Group
Carmelite House
50 Victoria Embankment
London EC4Y 0DZ

An Hachette UK Company
www.hachette.co.uk

www.littlebrown.co.uk

Out of the universal substance, as out of wax,
Nature fashions a colt, then breaks him up and
uses the material to form a tree, and after that a
man, and next some other thing; and not one of
these endures for more than a brief span.

Marcus Aurelius, *Meditations*, VII, 23

CONTENTS

I

'THE NORTH SHORE'
/the first part

We were beneath a shadow. From the moment I opened the curtains and saw that the sky was heavy and so very close I knew that another storm was coming. Swollen clouds, grey and purple, ominous, were massing out over the sea. The weak old sun could barely struggle above the horizon. The light was weary and, even then, even at the beginning of the day, it felt like dusk. Even then, it felt like the end of the day.

At noon, Mother left to go to the hospital, thirty miles inland as the crow flies, to watch Gramper die. There were tears in her eyes, and in mine too, as she kissed me goodbye. Looking back, it seems strange that I did not go with her. But we had listened to the weather forecast the day before and so she bade me stay and take care of things. Of course, she was also trying to protect me.

I watched her make her way up the hill, a small, neat woman with cropped grey hair. The heavy clouds hung above like dark thoughts. The light was silvery and flickered like a faulty bulb. I wanted to walk beside her and take her arm, to hold her up, to support her, but there was nothing I could do. She would never have let me.

After she had gone, I lay quite still on the couch in the darkened parlour, listening to the singing of the wind and the birds crying in the trees, my thoughts a spinning carousel. I could not stop thinking about Gramper, who had always been so kind to me, and about Mother too. I hoped he would not be in too much pain. I hoped it might even be gentle.

When I went into the yard to get wood for the fire, I saw that the sky was a strange colour, like a two-day-old bruise. The birds had fallen silent. I walked out into the lane and looked down the hill. Everything had become quiet and still. It was as if the land was holding its breath and waiting. Curious, I walked up the road to the church and sat on my favourite bench. From that high graveyard perch, I could see everything.

Inland, behind me, was the King's Heath: spiked masses of yellow gorse; drifts of broken orange bracken; tall pines, lonely and austere; and deep blue woods filled with cold, damp air and the perfume of leaf mould and decay. The road that Mother had walked up cut through the heath and then passed out of view. When it reached the forest that lay on the other side it dropped down to the River Salt and met the road to Dark Creake and it was at the crossroads there that she would have waited for the bus.

Below me, looking east and north, I could see for miles: the saltwater marshes, the coast road, the shingle banks and beyond that the endless sea, the same hard colour as the knapped flints the old church tower was built from. There were no boats out there, only a mounting bank of cloud, a wall of shadow.

I retreated.

By five it had started raining. The air filled with the scent of wet earth. The downpour soon became heavy and puddles began to form in the yard. I stoked the fire. It had grown colder, and as the light went from the sky I could hear the wind getting stronger.

By six a horde of devils were howling through the trees around the house. The rain came in waves and battered the windows. Looking out, the universe had begun to dissolve.

Streams of water poured down the glass, blurring my view of the garden and the world beyond. I kept the fire going and stayed close. For a while I enjoyed the agreeable sensation of being inside, dry and warm and safe, while outside the storm flayed the world. But between the rolls of thunder I could hear a persistent banging and so eventually I put on a coat and went out into the yard with a torch. The sound was the front gate being driven back and forth by the wind, slamming against the posts. By the time I reached it I was soaked, and my hair was slicked to my face and neck. The noise of the storm was incredible. Deafening explosions in the sky came one after another in quick succession. I could not but be impressed by the spectacle and went out into the lane where I was lashed with debris, twigs and grit being driven up the hill before the oncoming maelstrom. Sheets of water were coming out of the sky. A huge crack of thunder burst somewhere overhead, lighting up a world turned topsy-turvy. I saw broken birds tumbling through the sky upon scraps of light. The very ground beneath me seemed to pitch and lurch and I thought that if it was like this on land, what must it be like out there upon the open sea, in that never-ending darkness? I secured the gate and ran back to the house.

Shivering and fumbling, I quickly got into some dry clothes. And then the power lines crossing the heath must have come down. The house was dark. I was alone.

You don't pass through this land on the way to anywhere else. It is, in a very literal sense, the end of the road. That road brings you to the sea and then the only way on is to follow it north as it curves around the edge of the land, with the marshes, shingle banks and water to your right, the heaths, woods and fields rolling gently to the left, and the endless sky above and beyond. Sooner or later that road comes to an end as well, and then there is nothing.

On the North Shore it can feel that Scandinavia, or even the white void of the Arctic, must be closer than our capital city (which lies more than one hundred miles to the south in what is, to all intents and purposes, another world). The winds that bring the cold air in from the sea scour the land relentlessly. It often feels a great deal colder than the thermometer says it is. The sense of space, of vastness, is strong. It makes you feel small. At times it can be overwhelming.

In long winters the countryside presents a desolate prospect. When the trees have been stripped of their leaves and the fields have been turned over, bare of anything growing, it looks and feels like a hard land. Yet this bleakness has its own rare beauty. The famously big skies, more expansive here than almost anywhere else in this realm, are piled high with cathedrals of cloud. I say again, it is bleak, but it is brutally beautiful. I love it.

Yet in the summer, when the weather is good, it is another place completely. When the fields are full of golden corn, beet tops and lavender, and the hedges are thick with foamy heads of cow parsley, and the sun is shining, the land glows as if it is lit from within. That is God's light, on God's land, they used to say. Then people travel here from afar to witness this holy beauty. They come to swim in the sea and walk along the fading shore – on sand and shingle – and to explore the ruined churches and castles, the signs of a rich and complex past. Walkers and bird watchers love the wide marshes that are policed by fleet and nimble marsh harriers and home to an extraordinary avian miscellany: terns, warblers, lapwings, redshanks, pied avocets and the mysterious bittern, and even the gadwalls, goldeneyes and pintails that travel thousands of miles to this very stretch of coast, which for them is a kind of paradise.

Some say that it is a flat land, but they are really speaking of the fens, which are to the north-west, or the counties inland to the west. In fact, this is rolling country, cut across by little roads, much wooded. Villages crouch for shelter in dips and valleys, shadowed by ancient oaks. The people are tough and with a reputation for being distrustful of authority. On the coast they are fishermen, both for the haddock and mackerel that live in great numbers out in the deep sea, and for the renowned crabs and lobsters that live closer to the shore, which they catch from little boats using cunning basket traps. Inland they are farmers, growing oats, barley, wheat and corn, sugar beets and potatoes, and husbanding hardy cattle. There are many muddy pig farms. There is an unusual proliferation of both churches and public houses, which perhaps says something about the character of the people and the land in which they live, of the need for spiritual reassurance and a warm hearth where they can huddle together while the wind blows; bound by song and prayer and beer.

As the North Sea embraces this land, the storms that are visited upon us are uncommonly severe. High winds carry sea spray far in from the great emptiness, on air chilled by Arctic currents. Because of this, the people who live on the North Shore are hardy and ready. We build our houses and churches from flint, one of the hardest stones. Split a flint open and you might find beautiful crystals nestled among the opaque and milky planes. Split another and the shards that fall away will make good blades, unbelievably sharp if also fragile.

Gramper had, in the cabinet he grandly called his *Wunderkammer*, among all sorts of oddities and curios (including a piece of coral shaped like a lady's fan, a musket ball from the civil war and a dark misshapen stone, far heavier than it looked, that he claimed was a meteorite), a flint arrowhead. He said he had found it in his garden while digging for potatoes. It was a beautiful thing, pale grey but with a delicate pinkish tinge. Along the edges, where it had been finely worked into a series of tiny scallop shapes leading to the point, the stone was translucent. At first, I had taken it for a carving of a fish because of its shape, but when I handled it, I saw how light it was, and how deadly too, and I knew it was made for killing. I pressed the tip lightly against my thumb to test its sharpness and a spot of blood appeared on my skin. When I asked Gramper how old it was, he just shook his head, as if to say, older than you can possibly imagine.

Gramper also once told me that for the best and strongest buildings the flints must be small and round and that for fine flint work, such as on a church or manor house, the kind that is set so densely that the mortar barely shows, the workmen would test the size of each hard lobe by putting it into their mouths: a strange measurement.

The noise of the storm was overwhelming. Fretting, I put off going to bed and tried to keep the fire going and read a book by candlelight, but at midnight by the old kitchen clock, I gave in. When I pulled the blankets tight around me all I could hear was the house being pulled apart brick by brick. Tiles were being torn from the roof and smashing in the yard. Something somewhere was howling. Several times in the night I found myself wandering through the cold dark rooms, checking that the windows and doors were secure. I wondered what the best thing to do was, to stand guard or to sleep, but I had no answer. I worried that the windows would be broken and that the rain would come in and make everything wet. I envisaged the furniture, the carpets and Mother's precious books and papers – her hard-won translations, her magical works – all soaked through and in disorder: the beginnings of rot. The beginnings of an end.

I remembered then the stories Gramper used to tell me about the great storm of 1953. On that occasion, the sea defences had been breached. Many of the villages along the coast had been severely flooded. A powerful gale had been blowing for two days before the storm struck, bringing with it a massive tidal surge. As the sea washed into the little villages many people were forced to spend a bitterly cold night in the bare stone churches on higher ground. Gramper said that the devastation was such and the flooding so great that for weeks afterwards it was hard to say where the land ended and the sea began. The ferocity of the storm had been unprecedented, and there was something otherworldly about the aftermath. He said that the residents of Walcott had woken on the morning of Sunday 1 February 1953, ready to go to church and give thanks for their continuing existence, to find not only their houses filled with salt water, their possessions ruined and their kitchen gardens destroyed, but also a 4,000-ton coaster sitting high and dry on the beach, just a stone's throw from the edge of the village. Stranger still, the great ship was deserted.

In some of the villages further north the sea came washing

up the streets, pouring into the houses, carrying away goods and chattels, so that when the waters eventually receded it looked as if a strange cornucopia – chairs, clothes, pots and pans, books, cushions, pictures and so on – had, as Gramper put it, just dropped from the sky, as in that peculiar drawing by Leonardo. Weeks later, he told me, walking out into the landscape, he came across a solitary armchair in the middle of a sodden beet field.

Such things are difficult to apprehend. We make portents and symbols of them but always they elude us, or at least defy true understanding. Gramper said the great storm of 1953 was like *an act of God*, a phrase that came back to me that night.

All these things circled through my mind during that wild night. At some point in the early hours of the morning I must have fallen into a heavy sleep.

In the morning the fire was cold and the house was icy and quiet. I pulled open the curtains and saw a scene of desolation.

It was still early when I went out. Thick clouds crowded the sky, seemingly low enough to touch. The light was grey and pale. It is a peculiar thing, but looking back, I can remember no colour that morning. In my mind's eye I see the scene almost completely in black and white, misty like a faded old photograph.

A big branch had come down from one of the trees and lay across our yard. There were broken roof tiles scattered around and a dead blackbird, ragged and twisted, lay a few steps from the back door. Everything was muddy and broken and there were many large deep puddles. Although I had secured it the night before, the gate was wide open.

I went out into the lane. A faint breeze was blowing, bringing with it the smell of seaweed and wet earth.

With Gramper's stories still in my head, I was curious to see what the storm had done. I walked down the hill, along the narrow lane with the high-banked fields lined with ivy-clad trees on either side. Further down I passed the other houses as the village seemed to gather to itself, the buildings closer together. Eventually, I reached the Green, where the coast road meets the lane coming down from the heath, marking the edge of the marshes. It was still very early. There was no one else to be seen.

Everywhere there was debris. The winds had torn great handfuls of reeds from the marshes and scattered them all about. Many of the trees had lost branches which lay criss-crossing the slick tarmac of the road like a kind of ancient script.

It is a curious exercise to bring these things back.

Yet it is very vivid, even now.

I walked along the coast road a little way and then crossed the stile onto the wide track that ran through the marshes to the shingle banks and made my way towards the seashore. I was thinking about Mother and about Gramper. I was sure he had passed. It seemed to me that there might even be a connection between his transformation and the storm that had just swept across the land, as if it had borne him away.

I reached the shingle and climbed to the top of the high bank, my feet slipping and sliding in the unstable mass of stones. At the top I paused and looked out northwards into the great emptiness. Somewhere far out there, beyond the horizon, impossibly distant, were mountains covered in snow, vast glaciers and ice sheets calving into green water. I turned and looked back inland and I could see the cluster of houses that made up our village, and the small lane climbing the hill to the heath, and the church tower against the sky like a bleached bone, a skeletal finger pointing up to heaven.

We are small, I thought to myself. We are just clinging on, fast to a piece of exposed dirt, crumbling, at the edge of a vast void.

I loved that place even if, in the end, I was eager and ready to get away and to see what else there was in the world. Most of all I loved the marshes, those strange, wide, empty, cloud-vaulted places. The marshes are a special place, a world unto themselves, neither sea nor land but somewhere in between. That liminality is not merely physical, a border between the land and the water. There is something numinous there, a sense that the boundaries between dimensions are wafer thin and might be torn as easily as a sheet of rice paper. You feel it, if you are attentive; the rents in the fabric of space or even time that can happen at any moment. The burnished fox glimpsed slipping quietly through a hedge might be passing from one world to another. Just as the curious magpie is there in the corner of your eye but as you turn to look and say, *Hello, Mister Magpie*, he has vanished, is already somewhere else. He regards you confidently from a fence post, head cocked, as if wondering whether to engage you in conversation. The eerie noises and calls drifting on the wind that one cannot locate the source of. The sense that it is all shifting. The scrapes and ponds that move from season to season, as if possessed of a queer and unruly intelligence. The stands of reeds that grow and shrink and grow again. The huge flocks of birds that come and

12

go. In that border zone the mud – the very land itself – is always in motion, though to the naked eye it is as still as stone.

I was lost out there on many occasions. The first time, when I was very young, was terrifying. I was wandering and daydreaming, and then, without thinking, I followed an unusual bird call down a narrow track that twisted and turned through the reeds, their high furry heads swaying gently in the wind, until the way finally petered out. I could still hear that peculiar urging call but had lost all sense of direction, of where it was coming from, and of where I had come from. There were too many tracks to choose from and none of them were familiar; they all looked the same. And none of them led me back to the edge of the marsh, only deeper into it. The high reeds and grasses with their billowing heads meant I could not see in which direction the sea lay, or the heath, and so I became disorientated. A growing sense of panic built and I started to call as loudly as I could for help. But the only replies that came back were those of the birds, seemingly mocking me. I sat down and started to cry. Eventually that passed and I tried to push the fear back down inside myself. I walked and walked – quite possibly in circles or spirals – and seemed to go nowhere. It was then evident that I would die in the marsh, abandoned and forgotten, and that after a great length of time my remains would eventually be absorbed back into the mud and water, to become one of the spirits that some say haunt that place by night. But then I found myself on the main track, with the houses of the village and the coast road not far away. How I had got out I do not know. How I had been so lost when so close to home, I could not say.

Later, as I recall, when I was older, I would lose the way on purpose. I loved to find a small, enclosed space somewhere in among the reed beds, and lie down and look up at the sky, far away from the confusions of other people. There were little gravelly islands and small grassy openings, quite dry in the summer heat and protected from the winds and breezes, small spaces where the sun gathered. Often I would take a book. I could pass hours out there, reading or in a kind of reverie. I was shy and solitary, and with the exception of Quill I generally preferred the certainties of my own company. By then, I knew that I would always be able to find my way out, eventually. I was not afraid, though I knew the marshes could be dangerous. At school we were often warned of the perils that lay waiting out there. We were told stories of cattle caught in the black sucking mud, or cut off by the sudden rush of water into the narrow creeks at the turn of the tide, even of a man struck by lightning and burnt to nothing – a black absence, a scorch mark – by virtue of being the highest thing in such a wide and flat and open space just as a vicious storm came on.

The heath which lay inland beyond the village was another in-between place. A wild zone, very different from the marshes, it formed a kind of barrier between the village and the farms that lay further inland. Quite open in some places and densely wooded in others, it was a landscape of gorse and bracken, stands of beech trees, impenetrable masses of hawthorn, home to many kinds of queer mushrooms and innumerable curious small animals, whose names I would eventually know. It was another good place to get lost, another place to daydream.

Quill and I knew that young lovers found dark nooks in the bracken for their trysts.

*

14

In those days, I would sometimes spend solitary hours patiently wandering the shingle looking for curiosities: amber, finger-like belemnites and sea-shaped driftwood. In my searching I had discovered treasures as various as a tin whistle, the bleached hand of a shop mannequin (mistaken at first for coral), and nuggets of sea glass of many different colours, polished like beads. That morning, thinking that the storm might have washed up something even more interesting, I started to walk slowly along the beach, just up from the water, my hands pushed deep in my pockets against the cold wind.

I had my head down, scanning the ground in front of me, poking with my feet at the piles of rubbish and seaweed, the cairns of dead crab and knotted rope. I walked in this way for some minutes and at one point discovered a peculiar stone with a hole through it, which I pocketed. I later tied it with an old piece of hemp rope and hung it over the door to my room, for it is said that such stones – 'hag stones' they are called – are good protection against witches and evil spirits, though why that might be I know not.

I walked like that for some time, carefully inspecting the ground immediately before me, and then something made me look up. When I did, I saw a shape, just twenty feet in front of me. It was a dark form on the shingle, something heaped among the remainings of the storm.

For a moment, I thought it might have been a seal. I came to within ten feet of it and stopped. As I looked at it the dark shape resolved itself into a human form. There was a man on the beach. A dead man. A dead man lying awkwardly in a shallow hollow in the shingle. He was a crumpled heap of dirty dark cloth, draped in bladderwrack and tangles and haloed by dead starfish. He was curled up, coiled as tight as a man may be, his back rounded against the light, like a sea creature in a crevice in a rock pool. His legs were bent double hard up against his chest, but one arm was twisted out at an angle from his body. The hand was open, pale grey palm cupping the sky. I remember his fingernails, weirdly white, as if sea bleached. A thick coil of weed wound round his wrist and trailed down to the edge of the water like – a peculiar thought this – an umbilical cord. His hair and beard were long and ragged, matted and coarse, like rope and wool. His skin was lined and wrinkled, the skin of a rockfish, white and lifeless. Strange to say, but he looked like just another piece of wreckage washed up by the sea.

A dead man.

It was a dead man. As dead and still as a piece of wood.

I stood still looking at him for a long time. I had a brief vision of Gramper, lying on a hard piece of stone in a gloomy hospital room, the curtains closed and a pale sheet drawn over him. No more stories.

The keening gulls brought me back to the beach. I had never seen a dead body before and I hesitated. It was not fear that rooted me, at least not at first, but in my confusion it seemed that some kind of particular decorum might be required, a certain formality that would proscribe any form of intimacy, even if that was only to go and look closely at his raggy clothes and his bleached and blistered skin. As I stared, I noticed the way that his face was pressed awkwardly against the wet shingle. It then occurred to me that this occurrence – this dead man on the beach – was something I should report. But to whom? There would surely be some kind of official process to go through. With this realisation I began to feel scared as well as confused. I retreated to the top of the shingle bank, from where I could look down on the dark shape, and sat down to think.

A man doesn't just emerge from the sea. Like a bud bursting from the ground, he must begin somewhere. Nonetheless, it was perhaps possible that in the ferocity of the storm he had been pulled from some passing ship during the night and had drowned in the darkness, and that the currents had then borne him here. If that was the case, then surely his shipmates would have reported him missing to the coastguard or to the nearest lifeboat station, or the police at King's Eye. If that were the case, I should have nothing to worry about.

I had a small pad of paper and a stub of pencil in my coat pocket and I took them out and made a sketch of the dead man. Drawing is a kind of meditation and can sometimes help find clarity. I'm sure I still have that little drawing somewhere.

I tried to think what the correct procedure should be. I supposed I should inform the police or a doctor, or the coastguard perhaps. Then someone would come and take care of all the official business. But there was no policeman or doctor in the village. I would have to telephone, and I was very reluctant to take responsibility. I was somewhat embarrassed. There would be questions; there would be people to deal with. I was an age at which I was expected to behave like an adult, to deal confidently with the world, and yet so often I still felt like a child, half-formed and unsure, profoundly doubtful. More than once the thought crossed my mind that I could just turn and walk away. But as I weighed that possibility it occurred to me that someone might have seen me crossing the marsh. And if the body was then later discovered, my neglect would seem suspicious. So, I should do something. It was not possible to just walk away.

It occurred to me that there might be some way to identify the man and with that came the horrible realisation that I would have to touch him.

I went down to where he lay. The boots he wore were old and sturdy and made from leather, black with water and with nailed soles that were surprisingly clean. His heavy trousers and thick coat were both very dark blue but looked more like black in the grey light. His thick coarse hair was black and wet and speckled with grey. I bent down and gripped his shoulder with my hand. I pulled hard to turn him over onto his back and as I did a huge convulsion went through his body, a terrible spasm, and there was a great rasping intake of breath, as if he had just broken the surface of the water after a very long, very deep dive. His chest heaved and his back arched and his legs stiffened straight out and his arms twisted and his eyes opened wide – grey like the flints that litter the shore – and he stared up at the sky.

I stumbled backwards, sitting back onto the wet pebbles heavily, voicing several obscenities. I thought I would die. The surprise was awful.

I watched him, shocked into stillness. His chest heaved as he sucked air into himself. He kept coughing violently and his lips were flecked with foam and spittle. It seemed like something must be blocking his airways and he was finding it hard to get enough air into them. Then he was shaken by a horrible racking convulsion that passed through his whole body and he retched and retched and retched until he was filled by a taut silence. I thought he was about to vomit but no, it was a cough, an attempt to expel the blockage in his throat. And then it came up, a coil of seaweed, greasy with phlegm. He coughed the lumpish mass free, and it hung by its tail from his lips. He

18

coughed again and took hold of it and pulled and, like a conjurer who produces an endless chain of handkerchiefs from a pocket, tugged a grotesquely long shank of tangles up and out and with a distraught groan cast it onto the shingle.

Gradually the spasms subsided and his head rested back on the stones. Then his body was consumed by a terrible shivering. He turned painfully to look at me.

Our eyes met and I was shocked out of my appalled contemplation of that dreadful spectacle. I saw immediately that if I didn't get him to a warm place and into dry clothes he would die for a second time. Without hesitating I pulled him to his knees then put my shoulder under his arm and brought him to his feet. He was much bigger than me, but in my fear and panic I discovered an unusual strength. Straightening up, leaning against me, he coughed a thick gobbet of slimy brown spittle and looked at me again with bleary, unfocused eyes, as if trying to work out what kind of alien creature I was, and what I might want with him. Slowly, painfully, I started to manoeuvre him up the shingle. I had to hope we would meet someone coming out across the marshes on the path from the village, although after such a ruinous storm, what fool but me would think to go onto the beach?

It took what felt like hours to get to the road and we didn't see a single soul. The sky was rushing overhead. A squall of rain came down upon us and gave us a good soaking before passing on. We fell many times and, as I had to bear almost his whole weight, I was quickly exhausted. We didn't speak. There was nothing to say. Several times we had no strength left and collapsed together in the mud. He coughed frequently, great retches that shook his whole body and produced gouts of bloody phlegm, horribly spotted with blackish matter and pale spittle. He shivered constantly and his teeth rattled in his mouth. Our horrible dance, our awkward progress. We struggled in silence.

At the road I left him lying in the wet grass and ran to the Green. There was still no one there. I knocked on the door of Jack Newman's house but there was no answer. I knocked at the door of Bill Castle's house but there was no answer. The village appeared to be deserted. I ran across the open space to The Green Man but it was closed up and dark inside. No one came to answer my desperate banging on the door. It can only have been mid-morning but already it felt that the light was fading, the sky becoming heavier again. It was starting to rain once more. A miserable, heavy, unceasing downpour.

I would have gone to Quill, for she would have known what to do, but her house was in a village that lay some miles inland, on the other side of the heath. She was too far away.

I ran back to the man and saw that he was at the edge of an abyss, his eyes dull, sightless, inward. That terrible realisation filled me with fear and gave me further strength. I got him up again and we made our painful way up the lane as it started to rain even more heavily. To any onlooker we must have resembled two grotesque puppets performing a dreadful choreography, each operating the other.

Somehow, I got him up the lane to the house and inside. I left him lying on the floor in the hall, gasping and croaking, eyes closed, and ran back out to the yard to get wood. I lit a fire in the parlour as quickly as I could, piled it up with logs and coal, and then dragged him through. I couldn't lift him so I had to pull him along the floor like a sack of potatoes, dragging the rugs along beneath him like skirts. It was horrible to touch him and feel how cold his skin was.

I went to the laundry cupboard and carried down an armful of old blankets. I began to pull the cold sea-soaked clothes off his limp limbs. The man was slipping away and could offer me no assistance. His arms were stiff and heavy and it was a struggle to get the big coat, weighed down with salt water, off him. He was curled on the carpet in front of the fire and I wrapped the blankets around him. For all I could tell he was actually dead. Or at the edge. In a moment of inspiration I fetched the bottle of whisky from the larder and poured some into a cup and held it to his lips. He didn't move but some of the liquid went in when I tipped the cup. The fire was building up some heat. I could hear the rain beating again on the roof and walls and windows and doors. I carefully dropped some more whisky into him and took a gulp myself.

Then I went to the telephone. I wanted to dial the emergency number but when I put the receiver to my ear there was no tone. The telephone lines must have come down along with the power the night before.

I was stoking the fire when I realised he was sleeping. His breathing had become regular and deep, a wheezing, rising and falling, which seemed a register of safety. With the fire blazing, I looked closely at him. His face was creased, the lines etched deep. His skin was still greyish. His eyebrows extremely thick, like twists of wire, black and grey. Lips blue and scabbed. Veins and pores. Thick growths of black hair in his ears. Awful stench.

I quickly changed into dry clothes and then went to the

radio. I put it on but all that came was a cough of static, the sound of a world that had been disconnected. I didn't want to leave the man alone so I lay down on the couch where I could watch him. Outside, the wind shook the trees and the rain battered the windows. Lying there, exhausted, I must have gone to sleep, wrung out by the effort of bringing a stranger up from the sea and into our home.

When I woke it was still only the middle of the afternoon but a gloom lay upon the room. I tried the light switches but the power was still out. It continued to rain, but lightly now, and he was still there, as inert as a corpse.

I considered what to do next. He would surely need some kind of medical attention. Aside from the whisky there were some medicines in the cupboard, but I had no idea if they would be of any use.

I wanted to get help, but I was very scared to leave him on his own. Nonetheless, something had to be done so reluctantly I put my raincoat and boots back on, took up a torch and went out again. I hurried down the road and again I could see no one, no lights in any of the houses. It was as if the storm had carried everyone away.

Down at The Green Man I banged on the door again. No answer. I tried peering in through the windows and went around to the back but all was quiet and dark and apparently deserted. I had really been depending on finding someone there.

Quill, I thought, *why are you not closer?*

It was raining steadily. It wasn't stormy but you could tell it was coming on again. It was just a matter of time.

*

As I came back up the road, fretting and worrying, to my immense relief I found another human being: Alice Fitch at her gate. Alice was ancient – I never knew how old she was – and because of this she was mysterious. Only once, when she was young, had she been to 'North Witch'. But the experience of such a vast, confusing and dirty metropolis had so appalled her she had never been back. She had never travelled again. For the last fifty years or more her universe had extended only to the edge of the sea and to the heath. Although, that is not entirely true, for she had read widely and was always keen to know which books I had enjoyed. She once said to me, *one does not need to see the world with your own eyes in order to know it.* She had a kind face and a ready smile. In the summers when I was little, she paid me pocket money to gather the sour apples that fell from the lichenous trees in her unruly back garden, which she then made into a tart jam and sold at the church gate on festival days. Now, as I came up the hill, I saw that she was wearing an ill-fitting mac and wrestling with an umbrella that had been blown inside out. She waved as she saw me coming and I went to her. I was thankful for her presence.

'Hell of a storm, wasn't it?' I said.

'A real blower,' she said, nodding vigorously. 'Where is everyone? I haven't seen nobody.'

'I wish I knew,' I replied. 'I've just been down to the Green and there's not a soul around. And no lights on anywhere.'

'Well, the power went,' she said. 'I had to get my candles out.'

She staggered as a gust of wind battered us. She seemed so frail that she might have been blown away over the heath at any moment.

'Are you all right, Mrs Fitch?' I asked. 'Should you be out?'

'I'll survive, thank you for asking. Seen worse than this, I have. I just came out to see how things have been left. Out of curiosity, you might say. Think it'll be coming in again soon.' She jabbed the point of the umbrella into the sky. 'And what are you doing out in this? And is your ma OK?'

I told her that Mother had gone to the hospital because her father, my Gramper, was not well. Alice Fitch nodded sympathetically. I said Mother had gone to say her farewells, *to take her leave*, as she had put it.

'But in the meantime,' I said, 'something really extraordinary has happened.'

Alice Fitch looked at me quizzically.

'I found a man on the beach,' I said. 'I found a *drowned* man.'

She regarded me curiously, as if to see if I was teasing her. Her small green eyes were sharp and bright.

'What do you mean?'

'I found a man on the beach, and I thought he had drowned. But he's alive, though only just. He's in a terrible state. I tried to take him to The Green Man but it was locked up so I took him home. I didn't know what else to do. There was nowhere else to go. He's there now.'

'Where did he come from?'

'From the sea.'

She shook her head. 'What is he, a merman?' Alice Fitch chuckled, but seeing that I did not share her humour, she fell quiet.

'I know, it doesn't make sense, but I think he must have come from the sea. He was coughing up seaweed. He was soaked through.'

'That's a strange business. Do you think he went overboard in the storm?'

'I suppose he must have.'

'Oh, Lord. Where's he come from then?'

'I don't know, he hasn't spoken.'

'He's not commie, is he?' Her eyes narrowed.

The possibility had not occurred to me. 'I don't know. He hasn't spoken. He's said nothing.'

'Well, what are you going to do?'

'God knows! I need to get help for him. He's in a bad way. I've got him in front of a fire for now. But I don't like having him there, especially with Mother away.'

Then, as we stood there in the rain, she told me, in a rather distracted manner, an unusual story about her grandfather.

He was a sailor and for many years worked a big packet, not a fisher but a hauler, taking loads up and down the coast between King's Eye and London and sometimes even round to the south coast. Sometimes further north too.

'One time they are coming up through the Channel. It's bad weather, very foggy, big swell, wind and rain and hail and getting steadily worse and as that lane is so busy – you know they do say it is one of the busiest in the whole world – they have all the lamps lit and the captain posts several members of the crew fore and aft to watch for other vessels. Visibility is very low. Everything obscured by a white veil,' she said, briefly poetical.

Mrs Fitch stared into the distance as she spoke. It seemed for a moment that the wind died down and everything focused on her.

'Then the seas get bigger and bigger. It's now almost dark and getting really very rough, like a fairground ride such as would put your lunch back in your mouth, with huge waves bashing against the boat and the wind whipping the spray so that it hurts your eyes and stings your face and suddenly a cry goes up, Grandad Billy has seen someone in the water. Of course, they think it's a crew member. One of their own. The captain quickly does a tally of his crew as he brings the boat around, a task in itself in such rough conditions for the waves are washing across the decks now and they are side-on to the swell. Everyone is accounted for, which is odd, as Billy is certain he saw someone in the water, waving up at him. Waving up at him, that's what he said. *Waving up at him.* That's mightily peculiar, isn't it? So, it must have been someone from another vessel that was somewhere close by but that they can't see for the fog. But there are no lights out there. Only the white air and beyond that the night. They start to scan the water for a figure but as they do a particularly large wave breaks against the boat and sweeps another of the crew off his feet and over the edge. The cry goes up a second time, *man overboard!*

'They spend an age going in circles trying to find the second man in the water but there is no one to be seen amid the turmoil of the sea. One man lost or two? And would they have lost the second if they hadn't stopped and come about in order to get the first?'

She gazed out towards the sea, then continued. 'It lay on his conscience for the rest of his life. He swore he had seen someone *waving* up at him from the water. But he must have wondered if he had been somehow deceived, or even imagined it.'

She paused again. 'I'm sorry. Don't mind me. I do love those strange old stories he used to tell me.' She paused. 'And now you've got your own one to deal with.'

She looked sad. For a long time after I heard that story I wondered (and still wonder) what happens; if a man gets washed overboard out there, where does he end up? Does he keep swimming, desperately pursuing the wake as the ship moves ever further away, if he can even see it from within the deep canyons of the heaving sea? With time his strength will surely fail. And what then? Does he sink down and hang low in the darkness? Do the sea mosses and weeds gradually turn him into a swaying effigy, an underwater Jack-in-the-Green? Or does he stay by the surface and come this way and that way with the tides and currents, like a piece of flotsam? Would he be broken up with time? Does he come apart? Does he come ashore somewhere or does he find his way out into the great ocean, never to be seen again?

The man I had found had come ashore on the shingle and he was in one piece. But who knew how long he had been in the water.

When Alice Fitch told her grandfather's story I was transfixed, despite the circumstances. Her tale suggested a weird connection across time.

'Did they find anyone?' I asked.

'Not one, not two, nobody,' she said. 'Isn't that odd?'

For a long moment we stood there in silence, both picturing the scene, and then she said, finally, 'I'm sorry, I mustn't hold you. I can't help you. You must keep him warm and you need to feed him until you can get some help. Have you provisions?'

I nodded.

'You can come and get some fresh bread in a bit, if you like. It's just baking now. There'll be someone back at the pub soon, I should think. That'll be your best bet. You go back down there in an hour or so and get help. They've probably been helping the boats or clearing the road. It was such a blower there's sure to be work to be done. And it's coming on again, you'll see.'

I nodded again and she turned and slowly went back up the path to her little house. I went up the hill to our place, as the rain gradually increased in weight and persistence and the wind grew stronger and the light faded from the sky once more.

One thing at a time, I thought. I put more wood on the fire and then, leaving the man lying there before it, I went to the kitchen and made sweet tea and warmed some beans in a pan.

Then I came back, and I shook him, and he woke.

I was scared of two possible scenarios at that moment. The first was that he would either wake in a rage or a panic, and in confusion or anger lash out at me. The second was that he simply would not wake at all and would forever remain a cold corpse, pretending to breathe and sleep on the floor of our parlour.

But, no, he woke, softly.

He was quiet for a bit. Then slowly surfacing as I shook him again, gently. Coming up from the depths. His old grey eyes opened. Cloudy. For a moment he was confused and then he sat up and looked around. He was glad of the fire, I could see that. He was glad of the food when I offered it to him. He started straight in.

'Are you all right?' I asked, carefully.

He considered me vaguely.

'What happened to you?' I asked, enunciating every syllable.

No answer. There was a silence and again I was at a loss as to what to do. I could hear the wind outside and the steady drip of water. The logs cracked and shifted in the fireplace.

I told him my name, tapping my chest with a finger.

He looked at me warily but didn't say anything. I repeated my name but I couldn't be sure that he understood what I was saying. Perhaps he did not speak English. Almost certainly.

The sea could have brought him from almost anywhere in the world, I thought.

He drank the tea. Then I filled his cup with the whisky and that went quickly. The bottle was empty. It had been Father's, and Mother had, I suppose, only kept it for medicinal use, for she didn't drink. Or perhaps it was for her a sort of talisman to draw Father back from wherever he had gone? For it had not been so long at that time.

He closed his eyes and I thought again that I needed to get him to The Green Man but could not see how that was to be achieved.

At least he no longer appeared to be dying.

His clothes were still damp and cold. I went to the wardrobe and with a pang I got some of Father's old things: a shirt, woollen socks, a thick sweater. When I spoke to the man he looked at me, uncomprehending, so I laid out the clothes and mimed that he should put them on.

He considered this possibility for a while before nodding.

He pulled off his wet clothes wearily and stiffly, and with a great deal of huffing and puffing and pausing for rest, he put Father's dry clothes on. I watched him carefully. He didn't hide from me and I couldn't help but see and be fascinated. His body was old but still tautly muscled, tendons bunched like coils of old rope, weathered and bent like a gnarled tree. His limbs were blotched with cold, tracked with scars and densely ornamented with extraordinary tattoos.

On his arms I could see anchors, stars, daggers, dice, birds and many other things besides, including crude writing and cursive script, none of which was intelligible. Winding in and around this mass of symbols was a great writhing of vines and roots. His hands were decorated too, even the knuckles – which bore a sequence of letters that didn't resolve into any word that I knew – the flaps of skin between his fingers and the joints of his fingers, each with crude letters, crosses, stars and suchlike. A spider's web articulated each elbow.

Across his chest and torso he wore a great ship, a galleon in full sail, with swallows in attendance. Covering his back was a great black sun that rippled and shimmered as he moved.

As he pulled on the woollen socks I saw that he had a large cross tattooed on the sole of each foot.

Even broken, battered, drowned and almost dead, he was an impressive figure, and I was afraid of his coiled strength. We are told all our young lives to be careful of strangers and here was one I had dragged into my own house when I was all alone. Although what else could I have done, given the circumstances?

The man sits down again and is rocked by a convulsion, then another, coming from deep inside. A huge hoarse coughing goes through him and his eyes look like they might pop out of his head. He grasps the arms of the chair, as if the force of the spasm might throw him across the room, and I think he might snap them clean off. He sprays spittle across the floor, flecks fizzing in the embers of the fire. And then the gagging cough, from deep down, *coughing coughing coughing* and finally something there in the back of his throat. It hurts! He grimaces. It looks unbelievably painful. A final tortuous push and it comes again, seaweed, bits of bladderwrack, greasy and fleshy, a vile tangle. A greenish scum on his chin. Drip drip drip. He sits in stunned silence regarding the odd and improbable stuff he has ejected from his guts. I too contemplate this grisly spectacle and wonder what on earth has happened.

The fire cracks and shifts. Another small cough. Another shaking, a tremble becoming stronger. More coughing. Yet another of those horrible vomitous exhalations and this time it is leaves, sodden brackish leaves. Yes, they are definitely leaves, possibly oak or haw, perhaps even laurel, slick green and shiny-black with saliva. Then follows a prolonged and ocean-deep stentorian belch – bringing with it the vile stench of the rotten sea edge – and then more leaves come up, and some bits of pulpy vegetal matter. The last hanging from his bearded chin like a kind of perverse ornament before dropping finally into his lap. The stink! His face is stained with greenish spit and he hastily wipes it with the sleeve of Father's jumper. He is stunned, as am I.

After this extraordinary performance there is a long silence.

II
KNOTTY ENTRAILS

The Tempest. It begins, as it must, with a storm at sea and the *direful* spectacle of a *wrack*, all conjured by Prospero's rough magic. Nothing is as it seems. It never is.

In the aftermath of the shipwreck, Trinculo, finding a figure prone on the beach, is confused. 'What have we here?' he says, 'A man or a fish? Dead or alive?' And he leaps to a very odd conclusion: he decides it is a fish, even if it is 'legged like a man', for it smells like a fish (and an old one at that). Yet, Trinculo notes, this strange fish's fins are more like arms. He bends to touch the figure at his feet and is shocked to find it is warm.

Nothing is as it seems.

Prospero's island is populated with supernatural creatures including the monstrous Caliban and a tricksy spirit called Ariel. Prospero has freed Ariel from long imprisonment inside a cloven pine, meaning that the spirit is bound to serve the sorcerer. Prospero gravely reminds Ariel of this debt and threatens to return him to that woody prison. 'If thou more murmur'st,' he warns, 'I will rend an oak, / And peg thee in his knotty entrails, till / Thou hast howled away twelve winters.'

The Tempest is a beautiful and mysterious play, much concerned with magic and illusions, but also the instability of that state that we call reality. It suggests that art is a kind of spell that allows us to remake the world with our imaginations; an enchanting and profoundly moving notion. Despite reading it at school, I did not see it performed until many years later and so it is that Prospero and all the other characters, and the island itself, have a very particular kind of existence in my imagination alone. The island is peopled by figures from my past, who *are* the characters. It is Gramper – transformed – who speaks Prospero's lines in my version of the play, and a classmate called Smith, who was born with a twisted spine and mercilessly teased for it, who is Caliban. The drama's action takes place among the marshes, on the beaches, around the heath and in the haunted woods of that lost place – the landscape of my childhood. When I read the text, and the scenes are enacted before my mind's eye, it is me speaking the lines of Ariel, the *airy spirit*. It is somehow right.

Threshold. Some stories are like hauntings. They fade, as they should, but they never really go away. Not fully. They keep on coming back. We find them in unexpected places: in dreams, trapped between the pages of a book or hidden within a fleeting glimpse, the call of a bird, the trigger scents of rosemary or apple blossom. Or upon the faint track across the unfamiliar field that you suddenly know you have walked before, but in another time. Or even the exchange overheard at the bar as you wait to be served, that makes you think, *I have spoken those words before.*

There it is.

Once the story is known, nothing can ever be the same again.

When I found him, there on the beach, as cold as a stone, I passed over a threshold. I was unprepared for what lay on the other side. How can it have been otherwise? I still do not truly understand the events of that day, and what followed. Looking back now, the mystery which touched me then is still essentially unknowable. But perhaps this is because I was at that time a mystery even to myself.

Back then, when I looked in the mirror, I saw a face that was no longer that of a child yet not quite that of an adult either. Before me was something indeterminate, unsure, a being I often did not recognise. Half-formed, I had reached that confusing moment when your body is changing, hardening, but your sense of self is still tenuous. You do not know who you really are, and you wonder if you ever will. Human creatures are fragile constructions and I felt paper thin at that time, as if I might tear at any moment. That like Prospero's wild illusions and allusions, I might in an instant melt into air, *into thin air*.

On good days I knew that this is just how it is as we grow and change. But on bad days I felt doomed. I feared that the small store of certainties I had harboured all my short life was evaporating. That disaster was imminent.

This story begins with a tempest. And a body. In the first days of a new decade, three powerful storms were visited upon the North Shore in quick succession. The first was bad and many trees were brought down. The second was worse and there was much flooding along the coast. But it was the third, a wild upheaval of astonishing intensity, that was the most terrible. It was like nothing I had ever seen before. It left behind something very strange in its wake.

Field work. Time has passed. While I am not yet old, I am certainly no longer young. I already feel that I have lived a long life. Perhaps it is always that way. Time, which used to flow past so slowly, now seems to be racing by and I am rushing headlong into the future.

Many years ago I went to an art school in a big city but I was lost. It felt that I was there in the wrong century. I was not interested in questions of abstraction or the innovations of so-called Conceptual art, or the debates about Theory that were prevalent in the college's studios at that time. My tutors and fellow students scorned my interest in making paintings that recorded what I saw before me, or even the things that I saw in my mind's eye. The *process*, the *text*, ideas of *dematerialisation, participation* and *engagement*, they said, this is where it is at now. Figurative painting was then the most unfashionable thing imaginable. I did not finish my course. But when, after leaving and finding myself adrift, I began making obsessive studies of the plants in the garden of the house I then lodged in, initially as a way to root myself and recover a sense of focus, I soon realised I had found my subject, my way.

So it is that I paint plants. I am a botanical artist, or illustrator. I paint and draw flowers, trees and leaves, fruit, seeds and seed heads, moss, lichen and fungi. The wonder. There is no end to it.

There are two aspects, the scientific work and what I call my creative practice. For the former, I work with botanists and expert authors and produce precise and scientifically accurate renderings for illustrated *florae* and field guides, often either focused on specific geographical regions or plant families. My field guide to the flora of the shorelines and coastal marshes of the British Isles is considered something of a standard reference work. I made an extended study of the fungi of English woodlands. I have worked in the Pyrenees, in Tuscany, and

38

even Argentina. The work is rigorous but joyful. There is much consultation and discussion with scientific collaborators: what to include and what to leave out, how much emphasis to place upon certain physical characteristics (which may vary enormously from specimen to specimen). These drawings and paintings must be scientifically accurate and yet, of course, they embody a paradox. I am not a scientist. I am an artist. I feel that the images I make should have an artistic component, if only as herbs flavour a dish. They must look good on the page and be a pleasure to examine. I like to think too, that good work in this vein might capture and express something of the *character* of a plant.

While I enjoy the collaborative process involved and have even made some good friends, what I love most is to be out in the field gathering specimens and making detailed sketches before retreating to the studio where I can be solitary and silent as I work on the final illustrations.

Often people are surprised that I do this work, supposing that photography has replaced painting for such purposes. But photography has not made illustration obsolete. In truth, these two disciplines complement each other; sometimes I will use photographs as reference material. Nonetheless, it has long been accepted that, for the *definition* of species, painting is superior. A skilled botanical illustrator is able to create a 'compromise of accuracy': a composite image from several specimens, more generally accurate and less specific to a single individual exemplar. We generalise, and in doing so locate a kind of truth. We proceed from the specific to the generic. While each species has its own clearly defined characteristics, individual plants may vary enormously, and so photographs can be misleading. On the page, the illustrator may combine both face and reverse of a flower – just as we might turn it in our fingers in order to better identify it – alongside features such as leaves, fruits, seeds and so on, to give a comprehensive rendering.

The other aspect of my work is freer. I make paintings and prints which are exhibited in galleries, and sometimes even sold. In these works, I am able to invent. I can vary – even exaggerate – colour. I can idealise form. I can create impossible hybrids. The wonder. I use my imagination and create new worlds, new species, new realities.

The act of painting, the lovely slowness of it, the careful husbanding of an image into existence and the sanctuary of the studio, provides the quietness and solitude that I have found to be a necessary measure for the maintenance of equilibrium.

A grain of sand. In studying the plant kingdom, we become aware of the incomprehensible abundance that surrounds us, even when – paradoxically – the focus is on a single species or region. By concentrating on one small aspect of reality we can find a profound intimation of the whole, of the interconnectedness of all things, the flow of life. This is seen in Dürer's famous watercolour drawing, *The Great Piece of Turf* of 1503, a hallucinatory rendering of a small clump of earth from which sprout dandelion, softly serrated speedwell, hound's tongue, creeping bent, plantain and weightless meadow grass. In this modest image, a fragment comes to stand for the infinite variety of nature, just as William Blake contemplated a grain of sand and comprehended an entire universe.

There are other projects. Inspired by Dürer's example, I made an extended series of 'portraits' of plants commonly regarded as weeds – herb Robert, dandelion, knapweed, oxalis, viper's bugloss, thistles and others. In my paintings I rendered these aberrant but beautiful beings larger than life. With great care, hoping to achieve a kind of hyperreal clarity, I tried to elevate them to the status of the grand and the magnificent, which of course they are. I have often said that the mature seed head of the lowly dandelion is one of the most astonishing marvels of natural geometry.

But the project that is most dear to me is the dream of publishing a set of illustrations for Ovid's *Metamorphosis*, using Mother's translations. Her versions are wonderful, and I have the idea to set the stories in the present day, using settings from our family life. I want to render the details of plant and animal metamorphosis as anatomically accurately as I can – while at the same time acknowledging that such transformations are impossible. I cannot help but think it will be a kind of memorial.

The Sea of Tranquillity. What did you do in the war? I would ask. Which war? he would respond, winking and grinning. It was a routine we had.

During the first war Gramper had lied about his age. He was not much more than a child, and certainly not yet a man, when he found himself out in France, running mule trains carrying supplies up to the trenches. I loved to ask him about this; it always sounded like an incredible adventure even though he was at pains to stress the hardship and fear he endured. He never really saw action – never fired on another man, although the gunfire and shelling were sometimes uncomfortably close.

However, Gramper was gassed. Nonetheless, he was lucky, he said, whenever describing this most unfortunate event. When it happened, he was some way behind the lines and so the weird yellow cloud that came rolling across the blasted land, hugging the mud and the wreckage, was largely dispersed by the time it reached him. For protection, as he had been taught, he held a cloth soaked in piss over his face, but he still breathed some of the gas in and it blistered the skin of his hands and neck. That cloud was something he still saw and felt in his nightmares, he said. Because of the gassing he suffered problems with his lungs for the rest of his life. Not that it stopped him from smoking.

Gramper had all but given it up by the time I knew him, but still indulged in the occasional roll-up. *My special treat*, he would say. He showed me how to roll the tight little cigarettes he liked, and would sometimes let me do it for him. *It is the height of luxury*, he would say, *to have someone else roll your fags for you.*

After the war Gramper had gone into the merchant navy and had travelled far and wide – he loved to tell tall tales of those years. Then he'd met Granny and they'd settled on the North Shore, which was where his family had been from originally. In the second war he'd been too old to see active service.

Our garden was a mess. Father saw it as a purely practical space and maintained scruffy vegetable beds and a ragged square of lawn where we would sit on warm summer days. The rest was left to look after itself, which it managed perfectly well. After Father left, it all soon fell into a pleasing state of disorder. But Gramper's garden was a marvel. Neat and orderly, it was an expression of his personality.

He moved to be near us when Granny passed. I was still

a baby. The old photographs show that she was a handsome woman. She looked quite stern, though Gramper never neglected to say how wonderful she was. He lived in a small house on the edge of the village, one of three cottages on a lane that led up to the heath from the coast road. His house was the last in the village. On the edge of the edge, you might say. But close enough.

Gramper. Tall and thin, stooped in later years. Meticulous with his appearance (even if, towards the end, his jackets were worn at the cuffs and patched on the elbows). He would wear a tie to 'visit'. Shoes were always polished. His face was thin, almost aristocratic. He had a hawk nose, huge ears, filled with tufts of coarse white hair, and I vividly remember his bright blue eyes, which in his last years, when they lost their colour, became grey and watery, and somewhat opaque, as if clouded by the pale shadows of the past. A generous halo of fine white hair. A kindly smile for me.

When I was little, during the holidays or at weekends, I would often go to Gramper's house. We would play cards or do a jigsaw puzzle if the weather wasn't good. If it was, we would be outside. There were always chores to be done in the garden, leaves to be raked, seedlings to be planted out, veg and fruit to be harvested, and I loved to help. We would tour the small garden and Gramper would pinch some rosemary between his fingers and hold it under my nose. *Smell that*, he would say, *gorgeous, isn't it? That is the smell of the Mediterranean. A very useful herb, this one,* he would say. *Not only good in the pot, but, so they say, a protector against evil spirits. And nightmares too. Yes, put a sprig under your pillow and you'll sleep well and only dream of lovely things.*

I didn't believe him, but I tried it and it seemed to work.

This is another good cooking one, he would say, now picking a soft sage leaf and pinching it between his fingers to release the aroma. *You dry this one and burn it and the smoke cleanses the house.*

This is fennel. We hang it over the doorway and it keeps the witches out. And on and on. Mint, feverfew, thyme, parsley.

We would take the dog for a walk up through the woods to the heath and Gramper would bring his foraging basket. In spring he'd cut ramsoms in the woods and gather alexanders from the hedgerows; in summer there were elderflowers and then brambles to be collected; in autumn, field mushrooms and sometimes yolk-yellow chanterelles. In winter he would check the blackthorn bushes for sloes. And there were stories.

Nettles. *You know if you get stung you can make it go away by rubbing it with dock leaves?*

Yes, everyone knows that.

But did you know you can eat them? The Romans used to. I know, it doesn't seem like a good idea, does it? Well, if you do decide to make nettle soup one day, make sure you pick them before May Day, for that's when the Devil goes around collecting them and uses them to weave his shirts. After that they're bad, for he pisses on the ones he leaves behind.

Oak. *The father. You know that acorns protect you from lightning? Steeplejacks always used to keep a few in their pockets, especially if the weather wasn't looking too good. In the war, the airmen started taking them up in their planes too, imagine that!*

Lady's mantle. *Silvered drops of light-bright dew cupped at the base of the leaves. Alchemilla, so named for that morning dew,*

44

which appeared out of thin air, and which was so prized by the ancient alchemists in their attempts to create living gold.

We read in the newspaper that the Americans had crashed a probe into the moon, into something called the Sea of Tranquillity, which Gramper grumbled was an odd name for such an inhospitable place. The probe was called Ranger and its mission had been to photograph possible landing sites. My young mind boggled, and Gramper was strangely disconcerted.

Won't be long before there's men on the moon, he said, sighing. *H. G. Wells told it; I believe. Maybe you'll even get to go up there when you're older.*

Because he said it, I believed it might be true, that I might one day walk upon the moon.

Some time after that the first heart transplant was successfully carried out. There was a story about that in the newspaper, too. It seemed as though unbelievable advances in the sciences and new discoveries about life on earth were being made on a daily basis. I remember Gramper saying something like, *The world is not as it seems to be. Not any more. The more we know the less we know.*

He paused and thought it over.

What I mean to say, he said, *is that the more we know, the more we can see what we don't know.*

Do you understand?

I did, I think.

Transformations. Ovid is the great poet of becoming and was one of Mother's favourites. She worked on his texts not just as part of her job but for pleasure too. I remember her reading his peculiar stories to me when I was very little. We both loved them for their magic. Even from that young age I also intuited that they contained uncanny and potent truths. I still find them very moving.

From the first book of *Metamorphoses* we see tales of human beings, specifically women – it is almost always women – changed into plants or trees. There it is, for example, in the tale of Pan and Syrinx. As is usual for these stories, the nymph Syrinx is attempting to avoid the lustful advances of a male god, Pan, and in her desperation is transformed into something sexually unattainable. In this particularly surreal instance Syrinx becomes a bed of reeds, from which Pan then fashions his eponymous pipes. Is there not in this image a weird erotic charge, as he puts his lips to the hollow space and fills it with his breath, and an ecstatic music emerges?

The story of Apollo and Daphne is perhaps the best known. The god Apollo, filled with pride from his victory over Python, notices Cupid nearby and begins to boast to him of his prowess in archery. Tiring of his bragging, Cupid shoots Apollo with a magic arrow that he has enchanted to inspire love and ardour. He then fires a second arrow, which he has enchanted to have exactly the opposite effect. His target is Daphne, the beautiful daughter of the river Peneus. Seeing her, Apollo falls madly in love and immediately longs to possess her. He stalks her across the countryside, all the while boasting of his achievements and his godly powers and pleading with her to acquiesce. *Don't worry*, he says, *I'm not a wolf or a lion or even a hawk. No, I'm just in love!* All the while her rejections only serve to make him more and more passionate.

Finally, Apollo catches up with her, and in that moment

Daphne calls out to her father, pleading with him to save her, to change her from that which has inspired such insane passion. Even before she has ended her plea a strange *torpor* comes over her and she finds that her feet have become fixed to the ground. As her arms are transformed into branches and her hair becomes leaves, bark (or, in Dryden's version, 'a filmy rind') begins to encase her body. She is stilled, yet even transformed she remains enchantingly beautiful; Apollo can feel her heart fluttering beneath the new bark.

The story has been depicted many times by artists but perhaps the most famous is the sculpture by Bernini, carved between 1622 and 1625. In this overwhelming masterpiece, Apollo is rendered in the purest white marble, his lithe and youthful body garbed only in a flowing piece of cloth, billowing to emphasise the sense of movement. The sculpture depicts the precise moment when he reaches the object of his desire. Daphne, crying out, arms outstretched, is at the first instant of transformation. Delicate leaves are beginning to sprout from her fingertips, bark is rushing up from below to clad her form (and preserve her modesty) and, in an extraordinary detail, her toenails are extending and becoming roots that probe into the ground below her. It is an incredibly vivid vision of the precise moment of change and a miraculous technical achievement. With this superlative piece of sculpture, Bernini enacted his own metamorphosis, transforming stone into the semblance of living and moving flesh.

Bernini's sculpture is displayed in the Galleria Borghese in Rome. It is an astonishing and bewildering object, utterly beautiful. Some years ago, I was commissioned by a well-known gardener in Rome, an important breeder of irises, to make a series of 'portraits' of his special cultivars. While there I made a sort of pilgrimage to the Borghese and was not disappointed by that otherworldly sculpture.

However, for all its beauty and technical perfection, Bernini's work is not my favourite depiction of Daphne's *transflormation*. That hangs in the National Gallery in London and is by Piero del Pollaiuolo. When I lived in London, I would often visit the National Gallery and invariably found myself drawn to the gallery in which that small painting hangs. It is painted on a wooden panel little bigger than the sheet of paper upon which these words are printed. Daphne appears to be floating up into the air, a look of serene disinterest on her face; Apollo is clinging to her and trying to pull her back down to earth as if she is an unruly balloon attempting to escape his grasp. Daphne has raised her arms in alarm and they have been instantaneously transformed into two grotesquely thick and bushy branches of laurel. There is no sense of process in this depiction, no sense of a metamorphosis gradually spreading and overwhelming, as there is in Bernini's uncanny sculpture, and because of this, and perhaps also their curiously inert facial expressions, the image is comically absurd. It is as if a magician, Prospero perhaps, just out of view, clicked his fingers and – just like that – it happened. Seeing it, I can't help but smile.

Primavera. From Rome, having completed my iris commission and made my pilgrimage to the Galleria Borghese, I travelled on the train to Florence. That wonderful city was hot and humid and crowded, way too crowded. Around the popular tourist sites it was almost impossible to move. The noise in the market gave me a headache and the continuous navigation of bodies in motion, all packed together, was exhausting. Waves of Japanese tour groups wearing face masks moved through the squares. Crowds of football fans drank beer on the pavements outside the bars, waiting for a match scheduled for that evening. I headed into the Uffizi seeking refuge, but it was just as bad, if not worse. The galleries dedicated to the great names of the Italian Renaissance, Leonardo and Botticelli, were packed and chaotic. I had to use force to push through to see the paintings clearly. Just a few steps away the galleries of Dutch and French painting were quiet and subdued, and I rested on a bench in a room of sublime Rembrandts where the air conditioning made the air cool. I was in no mood for revelation but, despite the crowds and the noise, I still experienced something extraordinary. I stood before Botticelli's *La Primavera* and the world was stilled.

It is one of the most famous paintings in the world. It depicts a group of figures arranged as in a sort of frieze, arrayed in a forest or orange grove, or in a meadow or garden with a forest behind.

In the centre stands a solemn-looking woman with blonde hair, her head slightly bowed and framed by an arch of foliage. She is Venus, the goddess of love. She holds her right hand up and makes an enigmatic gesture with her long fingers. Above her hovers Cupid who, despite being blindfolded, aims his arrow at the group of women to the left. They are the Three Graces – Euphrosyne, Aglaea and Thalia – clad in gauzy robes that waft about them like wisps of vapour as they dance, and reveal as much as they conceal. One of them looks towards a man who stands at the edge of the painting, and we can tell from his winged boots that this is Mercury.

However, it was the right-hand side of the painting that drew and held my rapt attention, that bewitched me. Here is a group of three figures. Zephyrus, as blue as the sky, airborne, reaches out for the nymph, Chloris who, like the Graces, is garbed in ethereal cloth. She is fleeing and looks back over her shoulder at Zephyrus. Yet her expression is not of fear but of, if anything, a kind of anticipation. And as he takes hold of her, the extraordinary thing is beginning, and leaves and flowers come tumbling forth from her open mouth, as if the transformation is originating somewhere deep inside her.

Ovid tells that until this moment the world had been all of just one colour, a drab and monochrome place, but then burst into magnificent chromatic abundance. In her headlong rush Chloris tumbles forward and almost collides with the third figure, the woman beside her, who is indeed her future self. I find this notion of two aspects of a single being standing together utterly moving (and am reminded of the lovely line from *Alice's Adventures in Wonderland*, in which the heroine protests that there is 'no use going back to yesterday because I was a different person then'). Chloris has become Flora. Flora is wearing a most incredible dress, embroidered all over with plants and flowers which seem to be real. Where Chloris's fingers brush against the dress yet more flowers are manifested, or sprout, or spring, into being.

Ovid tells us that Zephyrus, in his remorse at her transformation at his hands, gave Flora a beautiful garden, filled with flowers and plants, a garden in which Spring reigned eternally. Perhaps the painting depicts that very garden, although some say that it belongs to Venus, that solemn lady, and that her gesture is one of welcome, a welcome to her audience and to me, standing dumbstruck before her and before Botticelli's visionary work.

There is more. Flora has bunched up her dress so as to carry a mass of flowers – pink and white roses – and she reaches her right hand in to take up a handful and is about to scatter them. Her face, framed by golden hair and flowers, is both purposeful and serene. Standing before her, spellbound, I am a still point around which the world silently revolves. The crowds and the noise have receded, have disappeared, leaving only this. She is the most beautiful woman I have ever seen and I cannot take my eyes off her. She, Flora, is the heart of this image, not the solemn lady who stands in the centre of the composition but is somehow separate from the action taking place on either side of her. I stand transfixed. Flora stares down at me and I stare back up at her.

The figures float. The ground and the trees are exquisitely rendered in incredible detail. I have read that more than five hundred plant species have been identified in the painting, with more than 190 different types of flower. It is a masterpiece of botanical illustration, as well as a profound piece of mythic storytelling. Despite the fastidious realism it is like a stage set and the figures drift before it, enhancing the narcotic quality of the scene. It is like a dream. Standing before it, I felt a rush of emotion, a giddy sensation, desire.

I later read that the painting remains a mystery and that even after all this time no explication is agreed upon. Art historians have argued for centuries over the identification of the various figures and the meaning(s) of the work, with no definite consensus reached. It may be an allegory of love, or of the arrival of spring. Even the title, *La Primavera*, was not given to it until the sixteenth century, more than a hundred years after Botticelli created it.

There is a mystery, as there is in all great art; the sense of something essentially unknowable. Yet despite the oneiric beauty, the sheer ecstatic weirdness of the image, and the brilliance of its rendering, those flowers bursting from Chloris's mouth always take me back to the moment that man, the stranger from the sea, retched a dark slick of leaves and seaweed into his lap, lit by a flickering candle, and the stunned silence that ensued.

Flood Warden. Now, at this time, somewhere in the middle of my life, I am witness to a succession of subtle daily transformations. The greying of hairs and the loosening of skin. The loosening of thoughts too, which meander in unexpected directions. I am unreliable and spin off on many tangents.

I am not who I once was, and I am not yet who I will be. We are all in a process of constant change, as is every object that surrounds us, from the fibres of wool and cotton that are woven together and form the clothes that clad our fragile bodies to the bricks that make the walls of the buildings we inhabit, the grain of the wood from which are cut chairs and tables and serving spoons are carved, even the clear glass that reveals the world: each single atom and molecule vibrating with hidden potential. We convince ourselves that things are not so, that 'stability' and 'steadiness' are states that we should aspire to. Round and round we go, blissful and ignorant, ever transforming.

Not so long ago, among the boxes of old papers from my mother's house, I found some curious documents relating to Father. One was a small notebook, dog-eared and dirty, with his name written in caps on the cover followed by the title 'Flood Warden'. I had not known he had such a job, if a job it was. The notebook appeared to me to be the result of long periods of meditation, watching and waiting, sometimes reading and – to pass the time perhaps – writing. For some reason I envisaged Father on the hill by the church gazing out across the marshes into the emptiness of the sea. Or on the shingle bank, crouched in that hollow where the dark form had lain, sheltered against the wind, patiently waiting. Inside the notebook were dated entries, mostly reports of weather conditions, wind direction and records of water levels. But alongside them were many passages copied down from books on watery subjects such as *baptism* ('a ritual death by drowning'), the *drowning dream* ('indicating a dilution or even dissolution of the framework of the dreamer's personality') and even *alchemy* (which, the notes read, 'interpreted the image of The Flood as a representation of the thinning of the self' and the Ark as 'a symbol of self-knowledge borne safely upon turbulent waters, a higher state of being, attuned to isolation and endurance'). There were lists of place names and of birds, presumably spotted out on the marshes, but more than anything else there were lists of terms used to describe water in all its various ways and states. Each list was headed 'WATER' and consisted of columns of words, thus:

Flux
Salty, Lapping, Sucking
Drowned, Cold
Drowning
Liquid
Washing, Flooding

Happy, Laughing
Chuckling
Pooled, Swirl, Swirling, Swirled
Torrent, Viscous, Pooling, Playful, Dragging
Flow, Flowing
Churning, Turbulent, Angry
Dangerous, Submerged
Calm
Briny, Glistening, Greasy, Chilling, Soaked, Roaring
Icy
Still
Dream
Changing
Glassy, Crystal, Hard, Hopeful
Unhelpful
Transforming, Pearly, Strange
Swallowed, Sorrowful
Deluge
Ebb, Flow
Opaque, Mud, Muddy, Choppy, Foamy
Obscure, Obscuring
Tidal, Cloudy, Flooding
Fluid, Molten, Saline, Salty
Disorderly, Broken, Swirling
Oceanic
Flux

I found this notebook oddly moving. *So many of those words could have been used to describe him*, I thought to myself. Somehow it cracked open the past.

Father was a man of contradictions. Tall and thin and, in my mind's eye, always grey haired, his skin browned by the sun. His face was like the prow of a boat, angular and impressive and pleasingly weathered. He ran a second-hand bookshop and read voraciously, but would have described himself as neither cerebral nor intellectual, rather as an outdoorsman and a craftsman. While he loved literature and regarded his shop with its teetering mountains of battered books as a kind of holy sanctuary, Father found an honest contentment in taking a boat out to fish or setting off to forage in the woods for wild mushrooms, or quietly whittling and sanding in his untidy workshop behind the house. Both places, bookshop and workshop, betrayed a mind that was unable to settle in one place, piled high as they were with books, magazines, tools and 'useful things'. His desk at the shop and his workbench at home were both heaped with sheets of paper. There were invoices and receipts but more than anything there were endless lists: of projects in mind, things to do and places to go. Plans and schemes. He was always dreaming up a new project: a table, a chicken run, a boat that he would build himself, the rescue and revival of an old cart or derelict tractor, the fashioning of new handles for ancient axes, spades and mattocks. His lack of focus enraged Mother, always so methodical, but it enchanted her too. Father could be good company with his endless schemes and ambitions, and tales culled from the many books he ploughed through while sitting alone in the quiet little bookshop, but he could also be taciturn and remote. He often retreated inside himself, especially at home.

Even as a small child I could see that they were an eccentric combination. The tale of their meeting had a mythic quality and was told like a mantra on birthdays and anniversaries. Mother, just back from Oxford, on a day trip up the coast from where she lived, browsing in the quaint little bookshop and then waiting at the counter to buy a foxed copy of the 1908 edition of *The Tempest* (now a treasured heirloom), surprised to be asked if she might care to go for a walk by the handsome and intense young man who served her.

She returned often to that stretch of the coast in the following weeks and then finally she came and she stayed. At that time Father only helped out in the shop at the weekends, but when Smith, the old man for whom the shop was named, retired, he took over as proprietor.

Mermaids. I open the newspaper and there is a report that the decayed remains of a 'mermaid' have been washed up on the beach at Hound Stanton, the crumbling seaside town which lies some way along the North Shore. The report says that 'gruesome images' show what looks like 'the remains of a human-like creature with a fish tail lying on the sand'. There is a picture and it is indeed a rather grotesque-looking thing, though more abject than anything else, with its hollow chest cavity and blank eyes like grey pebbles. Most people agree that it is just the rotting corpse of a seal.

It looks a lot like the pathetic shrunken remains of the 'mermaids' that I have looked at with curiosity in both the Horniman and British Museums in London. Tiny things, abject, desiccated, and deeply weird. In the Victorian period there was apparently quite a trade in such curios from the Far East, and enterprising craftsmen fabricated strange hybrids for an eager market, often using the heads and shoulders of monkeys and the tails of fish, dried and padded out and pasted together with liberal quantities of papier mache and gesso. The ones I have seen – black and shrivelled and unexpectedly small (for don't we assume a mermaid or merman to be of human scale, rather than the size of a cat?) – are clearly fakes and this new 'mermaid' looks something similar. It makes me think of how people are desperate to believe in something *other*. So much of life is dull, unexceptional. Isn't it so much more interesting to believe in the possibility of ghosts and spirits, to dream that mermen and mermaids swim in the sea, that a fish might be a man, that a man or woman might become a tree, as Ovid described?

For some reason I'm reminded of another of his tales, the account of Glaucus. In ancient Greek his name means *greyish blue* or *bluish green* and *glimmering* and he was a minor sea god. He was born a mortal fisherman but rendered immortal by ingesting one of those magical herbs that seem to have been so abundant in the ancient world. This herb caused an astonishing transformation: his arms became fins, his legs combined to become a fish tail and his beard turned green.

It was believed that Glaucus would readily come to the aid of sailors and fishermen in storms, having once earned a living from the sea himself. But those in trouble at sea could not always rely on such assistance, from either sea gods or fellow men. For it was also sometimes claimed to be unlucky to save one who is drowning at sea. The one who saves another will soon be lost himself, as the ocean must have its allowance. There is a quota of the drowned that must be fulfilled.

*

The Wild Man. *In the time of King Henry II, when Bartholomew de Glanville was Constable of the Castle at Orford, fishermen there happened to be fishing at sea and caught a wild man in their nets. He was handed over to the aforementioned Constable as a curiosity, as he was completely naked and showed human form in all his body. He had hair on his head but at the ends it appeared torn and split; his beard was prolific and like a pine cone and all over his chest he was shaggy and bristly.*

The aforementioned Knight caused him to be guarded continually day and night so that he could not get to the sea. Whatever was put in front of him he would eat eagerly. Indeed, he would take the fish both raw and cooked, but the raw he would squeeze hard in his hands until the moisture was drained and then he would eat it. However, he would not make any utterance or perhaps rather he could not, even when he was hung by his feet and most wretchedly tortured.

Although he was brought to the church, he showed no sign of respect at all or any kind of belief either by bending his knee or bowing his head whenever he saw any holy objects. At sunset he would always hastily make for his bed and would lie in it right up to sunrise.

It came about that they took him to the sea harbour and released him out to sea, after winding three layers of very strong nets around him. He soon made for deep water, and after freeing himself from all the nets he would emerge time to time again from the deep water and for some while would watch those observing him from the top of the sea wall. Then he would frequently dive under and after a short while emerge as if he was mocking the spectators because he had escaped from their nets. After playing in the sea for some time like this and when all hope of his returning had gone, of his own

accord he again came right up to them, swimming through the
waves, and stayed with them for two months.

But sure, after this he was guarded less carefully and was looked
upon with scorn, he secretly fled out to sea and afterwards was
nowhere to be seen. But it is not easy to establish whether he was
a human man, or some kind of fish displaying human form, or
whether he was an evil spirit hiding in the body of some drowned
man as is written by someone in the life of Saint Owen, particu-
larly as many strange things are told by so many about these kinds
of occurrences.

From the *Chronicon Anglicanum* of
Ralph of Coggeshall, Abbot of the Abbey of Coggeshall
in Essex 1207–1218, British Library, London

Flux. I have been thinking about that place, that attenuated
stretch of coast, the North Shore. Whenever I visualise the land
where I spent my early years, I see it in relation to the endless
expanse of cold water that surrounds it, that laps up against its
edges and alternately strokes it or batters and worries it, incessant. Beneath this particular sea lies another world, they say.
Not the sunken world of the lost villages – houses and streets
slipping beneath the sediment, disintegrating brick by brick,
flint by flint – but something much older and deeper.

The sea is like memory. Obscure, opaque, but always
moving. The surface is animated but below it are stiller waters,
slowly turning over and over, and yet more below those and on
and on, through layers and layers, and then the silted bed and
strata of soft sediment laid down upon the previous, concealing
and hiding what came before.

The land too is layered, and the earth and water perform an intricate dance. Water and earth: each is just a medium. Searching for the past, we dig down beneath the skin that is visible, through the roots and stones and down there, below everything is ... what? ... only yet more layers, more memory. Lost histories; like diving down through the murky water, a passage through the pages of an endless book. Here is revealed an inventory of place. A grave filled with bones and offerings. A sunken field system, long buried and submerged beneath dark waters, crawled upon by spiny crustaceans, cradling nails and coins, perhaps even a treasure hoard: the King's long-lost crown and sceptre. An ancient riverbed cushions a sacred ring. It rolls slowly along through liquescent gloom like a miniature wheel, pushed by gentle currents. All these things deep below the light, in lovely darkness.

There is so much that is unknown. They say that more than 90 per cent of the world's oceans are still unexplored. Who knows what is down there, in the deep trenches of the Atlantic and Pacific or below the ice of the Arctic? What memories reside in those inky shadows?

Flow and change. The sea, the land; in the end it is all the same. The bones will be washed clean and eventually carried out to the depths, to be ground to dust and add infinitesimally to the fine sediment that falls on all things in the deep. Eventually, with tectonic slowness, it will rise up above the water and become the land again. On it goes, on and on and around and around.

That vanished land beneath the grey waters is the source of the antler-tools, hand-axes and obscure seeds brought up from the depths. Once upon a time that land was not below the waves. But now it is. Along with all its history, all its memories. As we will all be, in time.

These images are always at the edge of my thoughts when I summon the North Shore to mind. Perhaps it is because I spent so many hours alone on that eroding shore, looking out to sea. It runs through my memories like the blurred letters that run through the sickly sticks of pink-skinned sugar-rock that are sold in the electric arcades and on the crumbling piers that themselves are falling steadily and relentlessly into disrepair, only awaiting the moment when they too will succumb to the inevitable and slip below the waters.

Strangely Beloved,

Your letter took me by surprise. How long has it been? So many years. Anyway, I knew your handwriting straight away, even after all this time. I've missed you, you know. Really. You're the only one I'm still in touch with, though we hardly are any more, are we? Must do better, as they say.

You know, I was always sure we would be the only ones to escape. The gravitational pull of that place is too strong for most. Certainly it was for our classmates. Only those with a certain velocity can get away from it.

I want to tell you that whenever I think of you – and I do think of you, more often than you might imagine, and always with great affection – I think of that first time I saw you, in the playground when we were six or seven. Even then I could tell that there was something different about you. I was the new one but you were standing all alone and it was like there was a forcefield around you. The whole playground was a sea of motion, of rushing bodies and noise, but you were completely still. You had a book in your hand but you weren't reading it. You were looking up into the sky and you had a faraway look on your face, as if you were in the middle of a beautiful dream. When I came up to you and asked you what your name was, you were shocked. I still remember the look of surprise on your face. You stared at me and I wondered if you were deaf or mute or just foolish. Do you remember? Eventually, we started talking, just rubbish really, but I knew then that we were going to be friends. At the end of the day, when it was time to go home, I asked you where you lived and you said, 'In the sea!' I laughed but I remember that for a moment I wondered if it might actually be true. That's how odd you were. But then you laughed and I laughed too and I think at that moment I fell a little bit in love with you. After that we were inseparable for a while. You gave me my name, it is the one I still use.

Do you remember, we used to sit together in class and hold hands under the table? I knew school was difficult for you. You were too bright for a place like that and they could not appreciate you. You were so different and no one really understood what that meant (apart from me, of course). You know, I think they were even a little afraid of you. Children are so cruel. I hated watching them tease you, but you didn't care. All the insults washed off you. It wasn't that you had a thick hide. No, you were sensitive and gentle and somehow permeable. But you had such inner strength and belief. You knew. You just knew. I always admired that. I still do.

What happened to you?

We lost each other, didn't we?

So much has happened. I really am an actress now. I still pay the bills by serving tables but when I meet someone for the first time and they ask me what I do, I say, 'I act!' That's something, isn't it?

It was wonderful to read your words and know you are still out there. But your letter didn't tell me enough. I want more. Unravel your mystery for me, please. Please write again and tell me what happened in all that time since I last saw you. Are you happy? Do you have someone?

Your postcards are still pinned up in my kitchen. It is nice to have them. Strange places I haven't been and will never visit. But I can dream about them and one day I hope you will be able to tell me all about it and what happened when you were there.

Write again.

With love,

Quill

Translations. The house was always quiet. When I think of it now it seems always to have been dark as well, in the sense that not much light got in, perhaps because of the trees that grew around, almost over it, and the creepers that clung to the brickwork. I liked that darkness, it created a sense of interiority, of enclosure, that was both calming and comforting.

I was an only child. I had Quill and enjoyed some company then, as I still do now, but I think I was happiest when alone. When Father left us, I told people at school that he had been lost at sea, and perhaps in some way I believed that. The truth was he had always been distant to me. He was not unkind, but turned inward, a person I sadly never really felt I knew. Eventually he simply decided he no longer wanted to live with us. He just went away. Mother said that he went to live by himself in the West Country and I had no reason not to believe her. For a while after that it was very hard for her, but she was stoical, as she always was. I helped her as much as I could. The two of us found a mutual equilibrium.

I never felt any need to be in touch with Father. Perhaps that suggests some kind of deficiency in my character, a certain hardness. While I knew he was out there somewhere it was in some ways easier to believe the myth of his 'heroic' disappearance at sea. It absolved him of blame, all of us in fact, and released me from the need to offer an explanation for his behaviour. When, many years later, I discovered that he had passed, I felt no real emotion, just a vague curiosity as to what might have happened to him in all those lost years.

Mother was always at home, usually in her study. She worked as a translator of classical texts in both Latin and Ancient Greek and did much of her work by correspondence. There was constant mail for us – work coming and going – and Mother often had to go to the post office carrying bundles of paper carefully wrapped in brown packing paper and bound with string. It was a journey we made together.

I would go and sit with her while she worked. Her tiny study was lined with books and shelves of card folders full of papers and files. It was a cosy and bookish place with a very particular smell. Rooms of books often have that sweet, musty, thoughtful smell. Like incense, it never fails to transport me. I liked to sit on the warm and worn red Turkey rug and lean my back against the chair in which she sat, tapping at her typewriter, her desk piled high with notebooks, loose paper and countless reference books. I would read or perhaps colour one of the many drawings of birds seen in the marshes that I liked to make at that time.

The desk was against the wall below the only window, which was half-covered by the ivy growing up the outside of the house, and so the light that came into the room had a glimmering, iridescent quality, *bluish green*, like sunlight projected through an emerald.

Liminal. It was a small part of the world that always felt apart, out on the edge, exposed and ancient, that was neither one thing nor the other, in a state of unrest. A part of the world that was somehow out of time, or beyond it, even.

Many hundreds of years ago there had been a thriving port. But over the centuries the slow movement of silt and sand and mud blocked the channels, and the changing contours of land and water and the fragile sediment it was built upon meant the town had slipped, building by building, beneath the waves. Then later the marshes shifted again. I had read that strange objects were sometimes disgorged from the thick mud, or were found washed up on the flats or on the shingle, artefacts of great fascination for the archaeologists at the museum: the expected old coins and pots, and clay pipes and bits of tile, but also the bones of obscure beasts, broken blades, teeth, things made from leather and wood (improbably preserved in the briny mud), pieces of amber with flies and beetles encased within them, coffin nails, flint tools, many abstract things of vague provenance. I had read too that at certain times, when the tides were exceptionally low, one could hear the tolling of the bells in the old church tower, somewhere out at sea. Of course, there are many such stories and legends along the coast, where villages have always been built on alluvial sands and gravels, where the land is washed away inch by inch, or suddenly in catastrophic storms, and the stones and sand redistributed along the sea edge. Everything is unstable. Famously, some miles to the south, there was an old church that stood at the edge of unstable cliffs, gradually crumbling. First the walls around the graveyard went, and then one by one, the graves themselves were exposed and the bones of their occupants tumbled inexorably into the sea. Finally, the church tower leant away from the nave and one night, in a particularly ferocious storm, it was dragged down into the water. For many years after that the nave stood open to the elements, the walls cracking and crumbling and patched with mosses and ivy. People came from afar to see this melancholy spectacle.

This coast is peppered with tiny hamlets that are the remains of once great ports and towns. A harbour silts up and becomes impassable. Roads sink into the softness of the sodden marsh.

The sea is another dimension, distinct from this one, as different as can be, and the North Shore is the place where two worlds come together. Yet that meeting place is itself subject to constant change, as one or the other element takes the upper hand: the land inching outwards or slowly worn away. The land fades into the sea and the sea shades into the land. Everything is threshold, boundary, all becomes liminal, all is contingent. Nothing lasts. So it goes.

Perhaps this is why ghost tales are so prevalent along this coast, because ghosts are memories that exist neither in this world nor that. Sometimes they come to us not as spooks but as objects, artefacts, remainings. The uncanny shifting of the land reveals secrets, lets us see back into the past, just as from the sandy cliffs at Cranmer a few years ago the skeleton of a huge mammoth emerged, as perfectly preserved as can be. Which tells us (so I read in the museum where those massive bones are displayed) that this land has always been subject to transformation, being at one time grassland or savannah. And on it goes.

Perhaps at some unknown time in the future it will be grassland again, and all that we see now will be buried and hidden. Or perhaps even the sunken kingdom of Doggerland, which once upon a time stretched from our shores to what is now continental Europe, will one day be restored and we shall be able to walk to Amsterdam without even getting our feet wet.

Does a particular type of landscape inspire a particular kind of story? I believe so. We speak of edges and layers. Of shiftings and changings. We speak of entropy and flux. The stories that spring from this land embody these notions. We might say that they *express* the land. For this place is inherently unstable. It is a threshold. It is the edge and beyond it lies a great emptiness. We project stories into that space. Tales of seafaring and wrecks and sailing off the very edge of the world. But we also tell tales of transformation and transcendence and they permeate the very air we breathe and sink into the soil on which we stand. How else could it be in a land like this?

Apple Cross. *When John Black of Saxling was finally overcome by Melancholia in the long winter of 1709, brought on by his meditations on the Flood, and his despair concerning the future of Mankind and, seeing no possible way of continuing, killed himself by blowing his brains out with a flintlock, he was buried in an unmarked grave in unconsecrated ground, as was then common with instances of what was called 'self-murder'. Yet that is not all, for the grave was placed at the Crossroads where the way from Shellingham to Hound Stanton meets the Peddar's Way, a site chosen so that if John Black's tormented spirit should arise in the night it would be confused as to which way to go, and so hesitating and prevaricating, be confined to* *that place until sunrise and then forced to return to the grave.*

One final act was meant to ensure that the Lost Soul would not wander. Undignified by a casket, John Black's body was stripped and laid face down on the bare earth at the bottom of the grave and a wooden stake driven through it and into the ground below, so as to pin it in place. Rocks were then heaped upon the body and then earth. No stone or marker was placed to indicate the location of the grave. This was the usual practice at that time.

Now, in the case of John Black, something extraordinary happened. Ash or white oak are most usually used for such stakes, but occasionally tradition has it that apple (the fruit of which symbolises the Fall) might be used. On this occasion the stake was cut from seasoned apple wood. However, the stake must have had a Green Heart for it sent down roots and, nourished by the cold flesh and bones of John Black of Saxling, then sent up shoots so that within a few years a good sized tree stood there at the Crossroads, and indeed became known as a marker, so that the place came to be called Apple Cross, which it still is to this day.

Every year this apple tree bore an uncommonly fulsome harvest. A local woman noted this and one year gathered several baskets of the fruit and took them to market. There they sold well and were praised for their exceptional flavour.

And so it is that the Man begat the Tree, which begat the Fruit which was then consumed by John Black's fellow men, and they had Children. And on it goes, in a great unending cycle.

Anon., 'Notes on Crossroads',
The New English Antiquarian, Vol. VII., 1865. Quoted in
Matthew Child, *A History of East Anglia*, Jonathan Cape, 1949.

*

Flood. It is a catastrophe. The water is rising. The shingle banks have been breached and the marshes lost. Grey water comes rushing up the lane, wave after wave carrying a bewildering array of debris: books, bedsheets, hats and shoes, a walking stick, leaves and branches, a model train set, boxes of papers, chairs, a bird's nest containing five bright blue eggs. In a panic, I climb the lane to the hill where the old church tower stands silhouetted against a turbulent sky. The water is rising at an astonishing rate, subsuming everything, and it becomes clear to me that this is the end of things, that all and everything will be obliterated by this elemental tide. At the gate into the churchyard there are two small wooden boats. One has a mast but no rigging or sails. The second has no mast but there is an oar. In the stern of the second boat sits the man who came from the sea, in the same ragged dark-blue clothes he wore the day I found him. His hair is wild, and his eyes are bright as he watches me carefully. He sits leaning back against the tiller and grips the lip of the boat on both sides. He says nothing but there is entreaty in his eyes. *The water is coming, the water is coming. Change is coming. Change.* Looking closer I see that his fingernails have cracked and greenish tendrils extend from the tips of his fingers and have merged with the wood of the gunwale, splitting the grain. He is of the wood, then, and of the boat, too. The rising water reaches us and I have no choice but to climb quickly in, take up the oar and settle in the prow as the little boat is borne aloft and carried away into a black vortex. But is it me in the boat? I am watching this peculiar scene from high up, perhaps from the top of the church tower, watching through half-closed eyes, buffeted with the wind and pounded by rain, hidden in darkness. Where are Mother and Father?

III

'THE NORTH SHORE'
/the second part

The silence lasted an age. The man sat there, stunned, stilled. I watched him as the darkness congealed about us. The slick mass of seaweed and leaves. The spittle and froth.

I cleaned up the mess with an old towel as he sat quite motionless, the firelight painting orange shapes all over him.

The edge of panic. I must do something. I needed to get him to the pub, or to find someone to come to the house. I looked at him and saw that his eyes had closed. He was quite tranquil now. Recalling the struggle to get him here in the first place and the awkwardness, the slow tiredness of his movements as he dressed, I concluded that getting him down the hill was not a task I could undertake alone. I would have to get assistance. So, to the pub once more, with hope, again.

I built up the fire, carefully. Enough wood and coal that it would go for some time, but not so much that there was any risk of a log rolling off. Apart from the firelight the room was dark, and it was tolerably warm now. He sat quite still, eyes closed, breathing deeply, like a statue carved from an impossibly old piece of wood, incongruously wearing Father's old clothes. I considered whether it was safe to leave him alone in our house. What if I came back to find him gone and the valuables missing? In truth, I realised, there wasn't anything very valuable to take, only old books, so that was not really something to worry about. Or rather, it was the least of my worries. What choice was there, anyway? So it is, sometimes.

We go along with events as they unfold, as the actor follows the script.

As I came down the lane in the dusk it was beginning to rain again and I could see that there were still no lights in any of the houses. It was like passing through a deserted village. The buildings could have been ruins. Where was everyone?

The wind was growing stronger again. The lane was full of mud and debris and, when I stopped to take my bearings and let my eyes adjust, little streams and rivulets began to form around my feet. A great darkness was in the process of settling all around me.

I hurried down the hill and when The Green Man came into view I was greatly relieved to see a faint light coming through the windows on the ground floor. Over the door hung the sign, swaying in the wind. I had always loved the picture it bore and once copied it in a class at school. It depicted the fabled Green Man, a being half man and half tree, or perhaps in the process of leaving the former state and becoming the latter, or vice versa.

I paused to catch my breath. The wind rocked the sign and water cascaded off it and onto my face. I pushed against the door with my shoulder and went in.

The room was gloomy. There was a fire in the hearth and a handful of candles had been lit. Golden light flickered off the glasses and bottles ranked on shelves behind the bar.

There were three others in there. Lucas Hope was standing behind the taps, holding a pint of dark beer, talking at Jack Newman who was leant against the bar. Tobias Stone was by the fire with a log in one hand and a poker in the other. They all looked around as I came in, bringing a blast of cold damp air and a rush of noise with me.

'How do?' called Lucas Hope. 'Still with us?'

'Just about,' I said sheepishly.

All the panic, all the fear that had been building up inside me since I had been down at the beach, began to overwhelm me. It was a rising tide, coming up past me, breaking over me.

My voice caught in my throat.

'I need help!' I said, much too loudly. 'Something terrible has happened. I can't explain it. Mr Hope, sir, Jack, you've got to come. You've got to help . . .'

My voice was wavering, and I could hear it becoming high pitched and maniacal. I began to shake. Tears pricked at my eyes and I knew my face was beginning to crumple.

'It's awful,' I heard myself say faintly, feeling that my legs might give way beneath me.

'Whoah, whoah,' said Lucas, calmly, soothing. He came over to me and with a firm hand on my shoulder guided me to a chair by the fire.

'Take your time,' he said. 'We've all been in the wars. You take your time.'

I wrestled off my coat, hanging it over the chair where it produced a quickly spreading puddle.

Lucas poured a measure of brandy and brought it over, winking as he did so.

'You'll be needing that, I dare say.'

I nodded. The panic was slowly receding.

'As I was saying,' Lucas said, turning back to Jack, 'We're not through this one yet.' And then, warming to his theme, 'It's coming on again. You'll see.'

Jack nodded and inhaled from his drink. He was tall and lean with thick fair hair which stood up off his scalp when he ran his hands through it. There were wispy whiskers on his chin. His face was thin, and his cheeks were hollow, and his eyes were bright. He had a great ease in his movements, as if his ligaments were a little looser than everyone else's. Loose and lazy. Not long out of school, but already so much older somehow, Jack did a little bit of this and a little bit of that to make a living. He helped on some of the farms from time to time, went with the boats when extra hands were needed, did some painting and decorating and so on when required. He was always friendly to me, and to Quill, too.

Compared to Jack, Lucas was weight and solidity. A big thick man of advanced years, large head with dark hair and a fulsome beard flecked with grey. There was rich colour in his cheeks as one would expect of a man of appetite making his living serving beer by day and by night. By virtue of being The Landlord his status in our small community was greatly elevated; people looked up to him and came to him for help and advice. Which was precisely what I was seeking now.

The brandy was fiery and most welcome. It eased my nerves.

'Mr Hope,' I said, 'where were you today? I came down a couple of times to find you. Everyone had gone. Like they'd vanished in the storm. The only soul I saw was Alice Fitch and she couldn't help me.'

'Tending to things, like everybody else,' he replied. 'In my case, when I realised quite what a bashing we'd had in the night, I thought I had better get over to Edge Field to check on Ma, make sure she was safe. But the heath road is pretty much impassable, at least for a car. So many trees and big branches down. Went along the coast road which took longer than it should. It's flooded in quite a few places. Lots of houses have their windows in and chimney pots down. There's roof tiles all over the place.'

'Yes, floods and trees down all about,' said Jack. 'A big land-slip at Creake and the water's up to the houses at Thorny Cross. They're going to get everyone out from there, or were going to try today anyway, in case there's another surge. I was with some of the lads down at Black Pond this afternoon, shifting trees off the road where it goes through the woods. Looked like a bomb hit it.'

They drank. I wondered how to say what I needed to say. Tobias Stone finished poking at the fire and stood up. He was a small man, quite round, tidily dressed, with a layer of fine hair fuzzing a shiny pink bald patch. He had compensated for this by cultivating a lavish moustache. He did accounts. I couldn't imagine a more boring and unfulfilling way to spend one's days.

'Is there any news about the boats?' he said.

'I think they're mostly in,' said Lucas, 'There'll be the usual waifs and strays, the usual flotsam and jetsam.'

'The boys were saying that the lifeboat had to go out last night,' said Jack. 'But had to come back in again. It was just too dangerous.'

He drank.

'There's a skiff from the quay stuck halfway up the high street at Saltwell. The prow went through the window of the post office. And no one knows how it got there, seeing as the water didn't get that high when it surged. But somehow it got way up.' He chuckled. 'Perhaps the wind blew it up there.'

'Who did the lifeboat go out for?' asked Toby Stone.

'Don't know. Apparently there were some big ones passing through, not just the fishers. International. Might have been tankers. Or Navy.'

77

'Did someone go overboard or something?' I asked.

'Who knows.'

They all drank in unison. Remembering the brandy I took another sip and felt its burn in my throat.

'Lucas, do you think it'll be very strong again tonight?' Toby asked, pensively. Most people deferred to Lucas when he was in the room.

'Oh yes. Surely. Absolutely. Batten down the hatches and all that. We'll have a few more days, I'd say. Just got to sit tight. There's no power. This is the best place to be. There'll be more stragglers soon enough. No telephone, no radio. This is the best place to be.' As if to demonstrate his point he finished his drink.

Toby Stone nodded in agreement. 'Did I say that Vic has gone up to the church to check on things there? He was worried about the big window. He'll be down soon I suppose. As long as there's nothing wrong.'

'That window's been there for an age, it'll be all right. He needn't worry about that.'

I wondered why I hadn't seen him as I came down. We should have passed on the lane.

There was silence. The rain continued outside and a log shifted and cracked on the fire. It was as if a spell had been cast. I tried again to work out how to explain what had happened and then realised that all of them were looking at me expectantly.

'You calmed down now?' said Lucas.

'You're all right,' said Jack. 'Everything right with your ma?'

'She's fine, I think. I hope. She went to the hospital, she got away before the weather turned. But no, to be honest, I'm not really fine. Like I said, something really awful has happened.'

So that was how I began the story of how I found a man

on the beach. But the way that Jack, Lucas and Toby reacted surprised me. Yes, they thought it extraordinary that a man had washed up on our beach. But they were particularly concerned with where he might have come from. Specifically, they wanted to know from me if there was anything that might indicate that he was a Soviet.

'Where's he from?' Lucas kept asking.

'I don't know, I don't know!' I replied, exasperated. 'He was on the beach and I assumed he had washed up. I thought he was dead at first. Then I thought he must have gone overboard in the storm, from one of the big boats. That's why I asked about it before. Either that or a ship went down, and we just don't know about it yet, and he was washed up here.'

'How do you know he was washed up?' asked Jack.

'Well, he was soaked through. And on the shore right down by the water.'

'But it had been raining hard all night, hadn't it? Could he have just been caught out in the storm? Fallen asleep or something?'

'Don't be ridiculous,' snorted Lucas.

'Oh, I don't know!' I exclaimed. 'How else could he have got there?'

'And you're sure he hasn't said anything?' asked Lucas.

'Nothing.'

'I'm just worried, is all,' he said again. 'All sorts have used this coast in the past. You all know it. Not just the smugglers but the French, the Dutch and others. There are so many blind spots. If you wanted to come and go and not be noticed this would be your place. Back in the war, Germans landed here and then made their way inland. For spying and so on. You all know it.' He pondered for a moment and he asked, 'Could he be Russian?'

'Why Russian?'

'Well, I don't know. Who knows how these things work. With the current state of things.'

Toby Stone said, 'A drop off, perhaps? A pickup? Perhaps timed with the storm as they knew the police and lifeguards and all would have other things to worry about. They might have underestimated the weather.'

He paused, drank, and with a grin said, 'You know, this reminds me, in the war a dead German airman was washed up at Cranmer. Then a week later another at Shellingham, and then a third and fourth on the shingle banks by the marshes. They'd been in the water for over a month. Must have been in a truly terrible state after all that time. Can you imagine?' He grimaced and sucked at his beer. 'All members of the crew of a Heinkel shot down somewhere off the coast down south of here.'

'They say there used to be a German spy living in the lighthouse,' said Lucas. 'He used to signal from the light room to the enemy's boats out at sea. Given away by his radio transmitter.'

'No, no, that one's not true,' contested Toby. 'An injustice was committed there, I heard.'

'Look,' I said. 'I don't know where he's from. But he's in our house and I don't like it, I don't know what to do. What should I do? What should *we* do?'

'Well, maybe one of us should go and check him out,' said Jack. 'You know, make sure.'

'I've got to stay here for now,' said Lucas. 'Others will be coming.'

'I should really get back over to Creake,' said Toby. 'Mrs Stone will be worrying.'

'One more first?' Lucas asked.

Toby paused, and then nodded assent. 'Jack'll do it,' he said. He looked pointedly at Jack.

Jack looked doubtful, like he was about to protest.

'Please, Jack,' I said. 'Can't you help?'

He hesitated. 'All right,' he said slowly. 'Come on.'

Jack finished his drink, reached for his coat and made for the door. I followed.

We toiled up the road. It was raining hard again, dark, and terribly cold. There was thunder out over the sea and it came rolling in, soft and round and distant for now, barely audible over the rain chatter and the bluster of the gale. But it was coming closer. Turning and looking out to the north we could see spectres of electricity in the clouds. The sea would be a roiling nightmare out there. The road was a river, which carried along it soil and stones. Above us the church tower was a black shape against a different shade of darkness, high above.

Jack walked ahead of me, angry, swearing loudly, his words whisked away on the wind. He didn't want to be there.

We reached our gate and I led the way in and along the path. We went round to the side of the house and straight on in without bothering to take off boots or coats. The power was still gone. In the hall there were some candle stubs in a bowl and some matches which I located from memory. With wet and stiff fingers and some difficulty I lit one. The glimmer of light was terribly small and weak. I lit another and handed it to Jack as he came in.

'He's through there,' I said, gesturing at the door.

81

Jack nodded and looked around, and then took up a heavy walking stick which rested against the coat rack. He waited while I lit another candle and then slowly turned the handle and pushed the door inwards.

The room was almost dark. The fire had died down to a few glowing coals and they were the only illumination. It was silent, but for the constant background churn of the wind in the trees outside, and the man was there, sat in the chair before the fireplace. I was struck anew by just how big he was, and how solid. Like a carved thing, an old wooden god. His eyes were open but he was gazing unfocused into the glow of the grate, spellbound; he didn't turn to look at us as we came in quietly.

Jack and I exchanged a look. Wide-eyed, he nodded again.

Moving as if trying not to disturb a sleeper, I put the candle on the mantle and took logs from the basket and laid them in the grate with a little kindling, carefully positioning them so they would catch. Jack studied the stranger. Still he did not move.

Jack and I looked at each other. Neither of us knew what to do. Jack was frightened too, I could see that. I nodded to him, as if to say *well, go on then.*

Reluctantly, he stepped forward and spoke.

'Hello?' It sounded like a question rather than a greeting and drew no response from the craggy figure.

'Who are you?'

Nothing.

'Where have you come from?'

Now the man registered our presence and stirred. The logs caught and flames leapt up, painting the room with a flickering glow. He was conscious now and flexed his great hieroglyphed fingers on the arm of the chair, turning to look at Jack. Jack nodded in greeting, hopeful, and there was the faintest intimation of a nod in return.

'Where have you come from?' Jack asked a second time. He waited. 'We want to help you.'

'Yes, we want to help,' I echoed, quietly.

The man took a breath and, haltingly, like someone speaking for the first time, or one who has lost the power of speech and is only just regaining it, said something. His voice was deep and full but rough around the edges, cracked and frayed, and the sounds made no sense.

He paused, and appeared to be rolling the words, if that is what they were, painfully around in his mouth like something sharp.

Very carefully, he said something else. Two syllables, perhaps. I wondered if it might be a name.

He waited, watching us. And then there was more, a staccato succession of word-sounds, which became slower and slower, a rush of meaning that was completely lost. I listened intently but could make no sense of it. This cost the man a great effort and he let out a big sigh, which was followed by a harsh cough, and then another.

Jack and I looked at each other.

Jack turned back to him and asked, 'What's that? English. Can you speak E-N-G-L-I-S-H? What are you trying to say?'

The man shook his head and another wet cough rose up from deep inside him. He gargled and hacked, struggling for breath. When he finally stopped he grimaced and I noticed a small dark leaf stuck to his lower lip.

I said my name and tapped my chest with my forefinger.

Jack did the same. 'We want to help,' he said again. 'There's been a very big storm.'

'Were you in the storm, out on the sea?' I asked.

He looked at us, from one to another. All I could see was incomprehension. Perhaps he was a Soviet after all? I racked my brains for some word or phrase in that language.

'Tolstoy?' I said hopefully. 'Gogol. Chekhov?'

Nothing. Only those sad grey eyes like sea-polished stones.

'Are you *Russian*?' I asked, carefully. But this worrying word prompted no form of recognition either.

The stranger coughed again and something caught in his throat. A piece of seaweed.

'Jesus,' said Jack.

'Something like that happened before,' I told him. 'It was disgusting.'

'Jesus.'

The man was racked by a terrible fit of coughing and then spat a slimy mass of brown leaves into his lap, speckled with red and black bits, and white foam.

The effort exhausted him and he slumped back into the chair and closed his eyes. He settled there, as if falling back under a spell.

'Jack, here,' I said quietly, indicating that we should leave the room. He gave me his candle and I led him across the hall and into the kitchen, gesturing to him to close the door behind. The rest of the house was noticeably colder than in the parlour, where the fire had been burning.

In the kitchen, Jack pursed his lips and nervously let out a long puff of breath, cloudy in the gloom. The candles we held flickered.

'God, I don't know what to think,' he said, 'but I'm pretty sure he isn't Russian. That's something, at least.'

'Jack, why is he coughing up leaves and seaweed?'

'Well, if he's been in the sea, as you say, perhaps he swallowed it down, you know, along with the seawater. Perhaps he was drowning and he breathed it in when he went down but then he came up and was washed onto the shore?'

'But *leaves*, too?'

'I know, that's not right.'

'Not right at all! Unnatural. *Unnatural.* He's got to go to a hospital. Or the police, or—'

'But they're all busy with the storm and the floods and all.'

'So, what do we do?'

'We?'

'Yes, I can't deal with this. Not on my own. It's dark now. It's late. I'm scared.' My voice was trembling again. 'I'm really scared.'

'Look, I want to help, I really do,' he said. 'But I can't stay.'

'Why not?'

'I just can't. I should get back down to the Green and see where I'm needed.'

I was angry at that. 'You're needed here!' I said.

The prospect of a solitary night in the house with the stranger was terrifying me. I felt the stirrings of panic again and tried to push back against them.

'Jack?'

He moved towards the door.

'Just go then,' I said. I could feel tears coming.

'Look, I do want to stay and help,' said Jack, 'but I just don't think it's a good idea. He's not going anywhere, and he's not going to do anything. I'm sure. I don't think he's dangerous. Really I don't. He's harmless. He's all worn out, perhaps sick too. He can hardly move.' He paused. 'Look, I'll come back first thing in the morning.'

'Jack, where do you think he's come from?' I asked, quickly. He hesitated. 'From the sea, I guess,' he said.

'Really?'

He shrugged.

'Why don't you lock him in there?' he said, nodding to the door.

I didn't know what to say. There were too many thoughts crowding my head.

Jack went to the front door and opened it. It was still raining heavily and the wind was blowing hard.

'I'll be back in the morning, I promise,' he said with a sort of smile.

He buttoned his coat up to his chin, pulled his hood as far forward as it would go, and was gone, quickly vanishing into the swirling darkness. I closed the door, shutting out the noise of the gale, and stood there in the hall, thinking about what I should do next.

The man sat there perfectly still, appearing to be asleep. Quietly, I put wood on the fire and drew in the curtains. I closed the door and went out into the hall. Then I bought a chair from the kitchen and wedged it under the door handle so that it couldn't open. Taking the walking stick from where Jack had left it by the front door, I went back through and sat at the kitchen table to consider my options. I would have to stay, that was clear. I agreed with Jack that the man didn't seem dangerous but, even so, it was best to be extremely cautious. Despite his condition, he might do anything.

The house was darker than ever. The light from the little candles was weak and couldn't penetrate the corners of the room. I boiled some water on the gas hob and made tea. I ate a buttered piece of bread. At that moment I was very conscious of my smallness, my inexperience, my insignificance. I saw myself, as if from high up, sitting in the small kitchen, surrounded by the house, which was in itself surrounded by trees and hedges and then, zooming out, so to speak, the heath and the marshes and the village huddled into the land, and beyond that the sea swaying and smashing and churning, and the thunderclouds banked up thousands upon thousands of feet, miles and miles in fact, into the air, and then only up there, far above everything, a burnished silence, perfectly cold, lit by stars and moonlight and the clarity and solitude and peace of space. That was where I wanted to be.

I had fallen asleep sitting at the table. I didn't know how long for. The tea was cold. I went back into the hallway and care-fully took the chair out from under the door handle. It didn't feel quite right to stop him in like that, despite everything. Nonetheless, I didn't go in. I didn't want to risk it.

I made my way upstairs to my room. The house was dark and lit only by occasional flickers of distant lightning and the following tremors of thunder but I knew my way so well I didn't need a torch or the candle. In my room I lay down on my bed without taking my clothes off and pulled the covers over me.

I was unbelievably tired. At that time I was no longer scared, I think. Fatigue had taken it away from me and emptied me out so that now I just felt that what would be, would be. As it goes, and so on.

Time passed. Outside the storm built to a new crescendo. The wind whistled and moaned as it rushed around the eaves of the house, and the trees were knocking and groaning and cracking under the strain. The rain was black and steady and heavy again. I could feel the weight of it out there beyond the walls of the house. Great rolls of thunder came in wave after wave, from both close by and distant. I imagined them rolling all the way from the frozen North, over miles and miles of empty sea, past oil rigs like monstrous spiders and the occasional lonely trawler. Despite the noise of bedlam, I somehow fell asleep.

I dream that I am on a boat. On a boat out in the storm, a big steel-hulled ship – cargo, not fisher – and far out in the North Sea, lurching violently in the heavy waves. It is night. At first I'm on the bridge, observing all the quiet intense activity of the captain and the crew. From a position somewhere up near the low ceiling I look down on them and they are silent and focused and the purpose with which they go about their duties suggests a serious situation. The boat pitches and rolls but I stay stable, as if I am hovering, a disembodied presence, nothing but an eye. But then I'm out on the deck, forward near the prow. Gripping the rail tightly, no longer stable, anything but. We rock and plunge, battered by rain and powerful gusts. The deck is lit by bright white electric lamps but the light doesn't penetrate far out into the darkness surrounding us, which is all around and both above and below. We could be in space, there is no up or down. Dense clouds of spray fill the air. Shudders of lightning illuminate a desolate marine universe, infinite, implacable, inhuman.

I see something in the water below me. It is a man, a man in the water. I call *man overboard* as loudly as I can, but my small voice can't carry over the crashing sea and howling wind. I call again and again, waving up at the bridge where I can see silhouetted figures against the yellow electric light. But no one can hear me or see me, despite the lamps lighting up the deck. I look again and see the shape once more, a dark figure in the sea, in a momentary pool of light, but strangely calm and not struggling or fighting. He is looking up at me, waiting. I call again up at the bridge, *man overboard!*

The boat plunges down into the huge canyon between two enormous waves. The momentum forces me to my knees as she bottoms out and then pitches straight into the next great wave, a vast wall of black water which overwhelms the prow. It seems we are under the water momentarily and as I lose my grip on the rail there is no sound at all, a sudden shocking silence. And then I am over and in and churned by violent forces and as I surface sound bursts in on me once again, a deafening roar of water and air and thunder. For a moment I have a terrifying glimpse of the brightly lit ship, pitching and bucking as it passes by, out of my reach, impossibly far beyond my reach, moving away, into the darkness, leaving me flailing in waves as big as houses. There is no one in the water with me, is there? No, I am alone.

*

I woke quite suddenly. I knew straight away that something was wrong. The quality of sound inside the house had shifted. The air pressure had changed.

The front door was open. I could hear it. Coming downstairs with a torch I could see the parlour door was open too, and I knew immediately that he was no longer in there. At that moment a gust of wind caught the front door and flung it wide open with a loud crash; a squall of rain and air and leaves came rushing into the hall and I went quickly to close it. As I got to the threshold I saw him, out there on the path, struggling. He was lit by flashes of lightning, like a broken thing, an old wreck, writhing awfully, a creature of odd and impossible angles spread-eagled in the mire.

For the second time I went to him. My father's clothes were soaked through, the man's hair was matted across his face and he was covered in mud and grass; he appeared to have crawled across the doorstep and down the path, grovelling in the water and dirt. He was filthy and breathless. He coughed hard as I tried to pull him up and again a cascade of leaves came forth from somewhere inside him. His weight was too much and we both sank to our knees. Somehow, finally, I got him up and pulled him back inside. I struggled with him into the parlour and he collapsed on the floor. I closed the front door. Revived the fire. Got the torch and looked at him.

He was in a terrible state. His beard and hair appeared to have grown wilder and longer and thicker, looking more like coils of wire or vine than hair. But he also seemed to have shrunk inside his skin. It was loose and translucent and had taken on a horrible green tinge. Frankly, he looked diseased. There was a dreadful marine stench, of the rotting stuff that marks the high tide line and attracts the gulls and flies. He lay there, unmoving but breathing very hard, groaning occasionally, his eyes closed, oily water pooling about him. Again, as I had once thought before, I saw that he was like a stranded sea creature. He was surely in the wrong place, the wrong element.

Once again, I wrapped him in blankets. Everything was damp. I saw to my horror that tiny mushrooms – pale grey with black tips and eerie blue gills – had begun to sprout all over the chair on which he had been sitting.

The wind continued to race and wail and the rain continued to come pouring out of the sky.

There were still several hours before it would be light. Not knowing what else to do, I went back upstairs and lay down again. What else could I do?

Somehow, impossibly, I slept.

And this time there were no dreams.

I woke in that slow, comforting way we all hope for. I remember the moment very well. I was first conscious of the weight of my arms and legs and my head pressing against my pillow. There was a quietness. When I opened my eyes, I saw that the room was filled with fresh light and it was morning.

Through the window the bare branches of the trees did not move. All was still.

Gradually everything came back to me. I recalled the events of the previous day and night and it seemed to me that there was a distinct possibility that it had all been a grotesque and elaborate dream; that I would go downstairs to find a bright fire in the grate, Mother making breakfast, fussing about all the things that were to be done. But at the same time, even as I enjoyed that speculation, I knew that it was no dream; it had all happened. He was down there. I would have to face him.

I should wait; Jack had said he would come.

I could not wait. I should at least see if he was still there, and if he was still alive. I had a terrible feeling that he might have died once again.

Reluctantly, I climbed out of the warm bed.

The room was cold.

It was early, still only a half-made day. But it was a beautiful morning. The storm had passed and I enjoyed the fleeting notion that the world had been remade.

I remember very well the odd sense of relief on waking up, followed quickly by the sense of impending dread at what must follow.

It is vivid to me, as is what came next.

I know that elements of my narrative thus far must challenge the credulity of any reader, but the strangest was still to come. As I write this, I am concentrating hard, and all these things, these strange events, are clear in my mind's eye.

Very quietly, I made my way down the stairs. The house was filled with silence. I was acutely aware of the creaking of the floorboards and the stairs as I shifted my weight, of the heaviness of my breathing, even of the rustle and rub of my clothes, trying to maintain the precious silence and stillness that had finally fallen. The hallway was dark and empty and so was the parlour. There was no one sitting in the chair in front of the fireplace, which was grey and cold.

I was puzzled. No, *puzzled* is the wrong word. I was unnerved. I wondered again if I had dreamt the whole thing.

But no, the man's ragged and greasy clothes from when I first found him were there, damp and stinking, in a pool of rank water. The slimy grey-blue mushrooms had begun to sprout there too. There was a dark stain on the floorboards where I had wiped up the leaves and seaweed and spit. The cup he had drunk from. The empty whisky bottle.

The kitchen was also empty, so I went to the front door and opened it onto the brightness, half expecting to see him collapsed in a dirty heap amid the mud and puddles of the yard, as he had been in the night, but the yard was empty.

He was gone.

There was a lovely peace upon the world, after the wild dance of the storm.

I stood there for a while, perhaps still waking up; not quite knowing what to think.

Not believing, without thinking and certainly not understanding, I started to run headlong down the road, expecting to see him shambling away ahead of me. When I didn't see him on the road, or at the Green, I ran hard across the marsh, jumping puddles and dodging the mud, slipping and falling at one point, until I reached hard ground and then the shingle bank, scrambling up it. At the top, I still expected to see him – perhaps standing motionless at the edge of the sea, gazing into the far distance. Even, improbably, climbing into a boat, some kind of homemade skiff with perhaps a shirt or sheet for a sail, about to go back out there to wherever it was that he came from, to some long-awaited ship that had come back around to retrieve its lost one, but there was no one there and I fell to my knees on the shingle. Gasping for breath, I stared out at the empty sea.

After the hard breaths had stopped I lay down, my back pressed into the cold shingle stones.

I stayed there for some time, stupefied. I couldn't pull my thoughts into any form of order. The sea came and went, its soft hypnotic push and pull like the soothing sounds a mother makes for a child, calming away night terrors. I looked up at the sky above me. A flight of birds passed over, high up, moving on from the marshes, or arriving. Coming and going, as all things do.

Eventually I picked myself up and made my way back across the marsh to the coast road and from there back to the village.

As before there was no one to be seen, but that was hardly surprising on this curiously becalmed morning. It was still very early.

The church tower stood out against the sky at the top of the hill, God's finger still pointing the way up to heaven.

At the house I noticed the tiles that had come off the roof during the first night of the storm, still lying broken on the ground. I resolved to see if there had been any more damage but first went inside and made myself a cup of tea. I tidied things up, putting the man's stinking old clothes into a rubbish sack, and set the fire going again. I wondered when, or if, Jack would come. Mother too. When would she return?

And what of the man? It was beyond comprehension. Had he really come and gone like that? Had he just vanished, or was he out there somewhere?

With things in good order in the house, I went back outside and gathered up the shattered pieces of roof tile at the front, stacking them by the front door. Then I walked around the house, looking carefully to see if there was any further storm damage: roof tiles, windows, gutters and so on. The garden was filled with debris and there were lots of branches that had come down off the trees littering the ground. I pulled some of the biggest to one side to clear the way. It took me a while to realise that something was different. The garden had changed.

At the back of the lawn, where the grass faded into a scrubby area which in spring was filled with pink foxgloves and in summer with tall heads of white cow parsley, was a tree that had not been there before. A twisted, stunted, ancient-looking thing, perhaps only seven or eight feet tall, with a thick and sturdy trunk covered in dark and scabby bark. Short stubby branches, as if recently pollarded, and a few new shoots and leaves that had survived the battering of the storm. It was clearly ancient, yet at the same time there was something fresh about it. No moss or lichen discoloured its craggy torso.

I stared at it.

Incongruous thing.

It had not been there before, I was sure.

I was circling it when I noticed Father's old jumper, or rather some rags of what had been Father's old jumper, caught on a low branch of the apple tree that stood nearby, and some other scraps hanging among the weeds. An impossible notion entered my befuddled brain.

It was a queer thought which I couldn't make good; it was the wrong shape, ungraspable. I couldn't hold it and appraise it properly. Quite calmly, I went back to the house and took up a chair from the kitchen and brought it outside and set it down on the soft grass from where I could contemplate that strange new and old tree, that unexpected presence. I sat there for quite some time.

It was impossible, but it was the only explanation. In the garden there was a new tree. Father's clothes. I remembered him thrashing about in the mud in the night, barely able to stand. He could not have gone far. It would have taken him days to crawl back down to the sea.

Once the thought was there, it would not go.

Surely that stunted tree had always been there and I had managed not to see it, or erased it completely from my memory. But it was not possible. I clearly remembered lying on the grass on that very spot just this past summer, taking advantage of the shade from the taller trees at the back of the garden. I had been reading Ovid. The tree had not been there.

I thought of the fine tendrils of the roots pushing down into the soil, seeking the path of least resistance, curling around the pebbles and stones buried there, pushing downwards, and wondered how it might have happened and what might have gone through his mind as it happened. I remembered the strange sensation of pushing bare feet into the sand or shingle at the beach, the rough cold stony matter creeping between toes, rubbing against the delicate membranes there.

He had made his way from the house, but on the path, instead of trying to reach the road, he had turned about – I imagined him stumbling, falling, staggering – seeking the quiet space of the garden, the darkness beneath the trees where the earth was raw. In his distress and discomfort he would have pulled off the thick woollen jumper and the other things too. Perhaps he cried out, calling either to me or even to the sea itself.

In a bewildered reverie, I meditated on this absurd possibility. Did the transformation begin from without, originating at his extremities? If it had, his fingers would have first become extended, soft tendrils, green shoots, sprouting leaves and buds. I pictured growth even bursting from the tattoos that marked his body. As his toes sought passage into the earth they would have pushed through the old wet worn wool of the socks, parting the threads.

Or perhaps the change began within? I thought of the way he had coughed up first seaweed and then leaves and that it must have been working away from inside him for some time. I imagined his lungs and guts, coiled inside him like the roots one sees exposed in the earth, but lined with slick wet new green leaves. With a shudder, I remembered the green tinge his skin had taken on.

I imagined it started like an itch, deep inside. A small point of discomfort becoming a pain and then spreading; the transubstantiation of blood and lymph to green sap. Or was it possible it had begun as a diffuse feeling of pleasure, like the vague comfort of warm sunlight upon bare skin, before becoming joy, growing into a realisation of imminent transcendence! Then he would have been laughing!

What had gone through his mind? Did he even have a mind at that moment? He would have looked up at the sky through the flailing branches of the trees and seen the dark clouds racing overhead. The rain would have washed his face and poured into his open mouth, perhaps slaking an aching thirst and soothing cracked skin and broken lips.

Did the new growth break through his skin, like a new organism emerging from within the husk of another, or did the skin stretch and change, becoming fibrous and dendral?

Was it like a sickness – a building sense of infirmity and pain – or was it instead a surge of energy, a growing strength, a sense of being connected to a greater power, of being plugged into the earth itself, part of it?

There were no answers to any of these questions.

Only a singular tree.

Jack returned at around midday, looking tired. I was still sitting on a kitchen chair in the garden, lost in my reverie. He apologised that he had not come sooner and asked where the stranger was, calling him The Russian as a joke. I simply said that when I woke in the morning and went downstairs he had disappeared. I had searched for him but there had been no trace. I didn't say anything about the garden. Jack was both relieved and anxious. He wondered what 'we' should do next, saying that we probably had an obligation to report a missing person to the police. I said I didn't want to do that, it would only be trouble. I said he was gone, if he had ever been there in the first place, and that was that. I was dismissive of involving the authorities and eventually Jack shrugged and went on his way.

Mother finally returned late in the afternoon, as dusk was falling. She was exhausted and hollowed out with grief, crying a little when she told me about Gramper's passing. He had died the evening before, at what would have been the height of the storm. He had endured a long, slow and painful death, not knowing that his daughter was there by his side all that time.

Mother said a funny thing too. She said that when the final moments came she saw him change. It was like watching a figure sinking into a deep blue sea becoming ever more indistinct, fading. And then nothing.

We held each other for a long time and afterwards, with tea, we shared stories of the funny things that Gramper had said and done. Mother took out some old photo albums.

I had everything good and tidy in the house. She asked me what I'd done, but I didn't tell the truth. I made it sound as if I'd just sat out the storm in the house and that nothing eventful had passed. I told her about the roof tiles but not about the tree. I don't believe she ever noticed it.

In the days that followed the storm I scanned the local newspapers for stories. I was looking for a sign. I read the shipping reports carefully and half expected to find something there about a castaway or a man washed overboard, a person missing. But among all the stories of chaos and damage and hardship there was nothing. Property had been ruined, roads were still badly damaged, the floods were taking more time than usual to subside, some people had been hurt (a man was in hospital having been hit on the head by a falling roof tile, an old lady had suffered a heart attack when her house had been struck by lightning) and assorted much-loved family pets were missing. A baby had been born in a barn. But nothing of *him*, nothing of foreign ships or anything else.

After three days something happened which I couldn't help but believe was connected to those strange events. Just two miles down the coast, a whale beached itself on the shingle and died. It was not the first time a whale had beached on the North Shore, but it was the biggest one in living memory. It felt like a sign. Such events have always been rare. It was not the only unexpected or unusual thing that was found ashore in the aftermath of that particular storm. A number of barnacle-encrusted bombs from the war were discovered scattered along the sands at Hound Stanton and a disposal team from the Royal Navy spent days making them safe and setting off controlled explosions. And at Burnt Deep Dale, a grand piano, hopelessly broken, choked with seaweed, sat atop the shingle sea defences. The sea offers strange gifts.

The next day Mother came back from the post office and told me she'd heard that a scientist was coming from the university to examine the whale and to cut it open to see what might be inside. There might be something to explain why it had beached. He would be there the day after next. I resolved to go to the beach to witness that event; maybe there the key to this curious story might be revealed.

That day was cold but clear. The sky was empty of cloud and a gentle but icy wind blew in from the sea. I left early, wanting to be sure I didn't miss anything, and walked along the shore-line until I reached the scene. I could see the whale from quite a way off, an enormous dark mass lying across the beach like a barrier.

Closer still I was able to distinguish the flukes of the tail and its great block-like head. I walked closer again and saw its big eye was pitch black and liquid and when I looked in I could see no bottom in there. This was a creature that could dive down thousands of feet below the surface of the water – into unim-aginable darkness and density, hunting giant squid and other dwellers in the deep – it was extraordinary to see it on our shore. It was utterly alien, and completely unknowable.

The whale was lying on its side and there were barnacles on its pale, crumpled belly. Close up its skin displayed an amazing range of colours; in places it was a deep blue, iridescent and oily, yet elsewhere it was black like ebony or charcoal, especially where it was wet; there were also areas of soft grey, some brown like milky tea and some pale whitish areas, lined with long grooves, particularly along its underside. Below the head it was white. Some parts were smooth – as if polished – others were wrinkled like an old prune, rough and almost bark-like. I was amazed to see that all over it was cratered with pockmarks and long scrapes and scratches. It looked as if it had texts in ornate cursive script written along its flanks from its head to its great tail, but it was a text no man could possibly decipher. I estimated it to be some sixty feet long.

The tide had come and gone around it over the few days it had lain there, shifting the sand so that its great bulk now lay in a shallow trough filled with foamy seawater. It was an awesome sight. Seagulls stood atop its vast bulk, proprietorially, watching the massing humans carefully.

A few people were already there and as the morning drew on yet more arrived. I found a good vantage point out of the wind where the beach became dunes and there were hillocks and dips of sand topped by tough marram grass. Mother had given me hot tea in a flask and some sandwiches and I was quite comfortable, despite the cold. I had brought a small sketch pad and made drawings of the scene.

At midday a group of men came marching down the path from the coast road carrying assorted bags and boxes. They set everything down on the sand and walked around and around the whale, talking excitedly, and pointing and gesturing. After some time they took shiny rubber overalls from their bags and put them on and then started to unpack their equipment. By now there was a small crowd watching. They took out wooden stakes and drove them into the sand at intervals around the body, and then tied rope between them, to create a barriered area within which they could work. Several, who appeared to be students, began to make measurements with a long tape, while a third made notes. One peered deeply into the void of that big black eye for what seemed like an unusually long time. Another made a close examination of the great teeth that lined the whale's long and weirdly narrow mouth.

They then unpacked an array of cruel-looking long-bladed knives, brutal hooks and horribly long bone saws and went to work. One climbed on top of the head and started to cut in and down using a strange drill-like machine that looked more like an instrument of torture than one of science. Seeing that made me feel distinctly queasy. Two others took a great knife and started at the underside, cutting a line between the dark grey-black colouration and the paler flesh of the belly. At first, as they cut into the beast, nothing happened, it was like cutting a log or a stone, but as they cut deeper through layers of blubber and muscle, different coloured liquids, including a substantial quantity of thick dark blood, began to pour out, splashing their overalls, staining the sand and colouring the pool of water the whale lay in. Before long it looked like a massacre had taken place. Having made a long and deep lateral cut they then took hooks and used them to draw the lips of the wound aside, exposing the creature's enormous internal organs. A mass of guts flowed out of the opening, uncoiling like rope, bulbous pipes and tubes in an array of unexpected colours including wine-dark purple, pale blue, sickly green and sour yellow, as well as red and pink. Cutting further the two men reached the stomach, which they intended to open up. The crowd was drawing closer and I, too, walked down the sand so that I could have a good view. There was a sense of anticipation. An old man standing next to me nudged my arm with his elbow.

'I hope they don't find Jonah in there,' he said.

But when they opened it up there was nothing remarkable, just a mass of more or less digested fish and squid and the remains of fishing nets.

After that people started to drift away.

One of the scientists pulled off his gloves, ducked under the tape barrier and walked a little way from the scene. He lit a cigarette, blowing a cloud of white smoke into the wind, and stared out to sea. I went over to him.

'How did it die?' I asked.

He looked at me. 'Hard to say. Funnily enough – well, not funny really – it probably drowned.'

'Drowned?'

'In the shallow water. It shouldn't be here. It happens, but we don't really know why. They get lost, separated from their fellows, disorientated. Then they get stuck in the shallow waters. They're deep-sea creatures and they cannot cope. They can't deal with the shallows.'

'So sad,' I said.

'Yes, it is,' he agreed. He took a long draw on his cigarette. 'Once they're washed up and out of the water they are already dying really. Lungs blocked with blood. Organ failure.'

After a while I asked another question. 'What will happen to it?'

He smiled at me. 'It'll rot. It'll take some time but it'll rot down eventually and in the meantime the birds will feed. And maybe rats and mice and perhaps even a fox from the woods, if it's brave.' He nodded inland. 'Then depending on the tides it might move up and down the beach. Gradually it'll break up. The movement will speed that process along. The crabs and fish will feed. Insects too. Larvae, and so on. It'll be a real feast. It's nature's way. Life then death then life again. Transformation. The endless cycle. Eventually it will be gone, but for the bones. Some will wash up here and some will go out to sea. After a while, there won't be anything left to see. Of course, if there's another storm and high tides it may get carried away sooner.'

I imagined the dead thing, paradoxically teeming with life. Inert matter altered. Death consumed and turned into life. *So it goes*, I thought to myself.

He finished his cigarette and dropped it onto the sand, pushing it in with his toe, then walked back to the whale.

'The endless cycle,' I repeated.

The scientists continued to work, talking quietly among themselves, taking measurements and cutting away samples that they packed into the assorted vessels they had brought with them. Eventually, as the light began to fade and the temperature dropped, they took off their rubber overalls and packed up their things before trudging back up the sandy track in single file, like priests.

I was the last to leave. The whale had been most terribly violated, even in death, and I felt a profound grief for it. Its eyes had been cut out and placed in jars of preserving fluid. Some of the teeth had been forced from its jaw. The strangely beautiful and ancient script that ran along its long flanks was interrupted by bloody cuts where sections of flesh and blubber had been removed, samples taken from flank and fin and fluke. Now the seagulls came back, and some evil-looking crows, and started to pick at its guts, which were arrayed across the sand in grisly patterns and floating abjectly in the pool of bloody seawater.

It was as dark as the end of the world when I set out to walk the several miles home.

IV

KNAPPED FLINT

Ghosts. It was not how I remembered it. When I found the manuscript entitled *The North Shore* and read it I was surprised and confused. It was not how I remembered it. I recalled both the desperate discovery of the man on that wind-scoured winter beach, and the struggle to bring him to the house. All of that seemed right. But what happened later was, in my memory, as I had told it to Jack: I had woken in the morning and found the man gone; that had been that. There had been no tree, I was sure of that.

I recalled, too, the day I went to see the whale. The bright colours of its guts and the way the blood stained the sand are still vivid in my mind's eye. The melancholy spectacle and what had felt like the cruelty of the scientists towards a fellow being had left an indelible impression. Indeed, that day had come to assume for me the status of an augur or a symbol. Something of mankind's fraught and crooked relationship with nature was contained in that scene.

I had been moving house when I found the papers. A lot of books and pictures and folders of old drawings and files had accumulated over the years. I was filling rubbish bags with the forgotten, the useless, the broken and the unrequited and it felt good to lighten my passage a little. I came across a number of unfamiliar old cardboard boxes, sealed with yellowed tape, trying to burst open. These had been out of sight at the back of the loft for many years, accumulating dust. They were boxes,

I realised, which had come from my mother's house by the marshes, which I must have taken possession of when I sold her home after she passed away.

These boxes were time capsules; sealed fragments of a past that, I now realised, was both half-forgotten and half-remembered. Upon opening, I discovered they contained folders full of papers from another time in my life; there were letters and postcards, old school certificates and an address book with just a handful of unfamiliar names. There were some brown envelopes of old photographs, faded and yellowing with age. One contained nondescript views across the marshes on an unremembered sunny day one summer, another held scenes from a family holiday, camping somewhere: Mother and Father smiling at the camera (which I must have been holding) through haloes of flaming and flaring oranges, yellows, methylated blues and washed pinks. Another contained a miscellany of old family portraits in a range of formats; black and white, pale colour prints, uncanny in their lack of precision, fugitive polaroids: a parade of aunts and uncles, great aunts and great uncles, great grandparents, cousins and so on, whose names I no longer knew and whose exact connections to me were obscure. There were notebooks. A scrapbook contained yellowed newspaper cuttings and magazine articles: an odd mix of weather reports, tide tables, a well-worn library card. A shoebox was filled with childish drawings, some with crude inscriptions and dedications, evidently saved by Mother. Most peculiarly there was a sheaf of loose papers in a card folder, the handwritten manuscript entitled *The North Shore*. Between the sheets of paper were pressed a number of brittle brown leaves of a variety that defied immediate identification.

I glanced through it vacantly, not remembering it. I was about to bin it along with all the other junk when a few passages caught my eye, some almost-familiar names – Jack, Lucas, Bill, Alice – and, distractedly at first, but with growing attentiveness, I began to read.

I went through it in one sitting, skimming, and then, unsteady, poured myself a whisky before sitting back down. I read the text through again several times with an increasingly appalled fascination, quite oblivious to the passage of time. At first, I took it for a work of fiction, a fiction nonetheless rooted in my own life and that place that was so much a part of me. But then the slow realisation that this really was my story began to grip me, and the implications of that were deeply unnerving. I had forgotten the writing of it.

I remembered a version of the events described but even with the very words in front of my eyes, I struggled to recall putting pen to paper and forming those words, those sentences, that story. More than two decades had passed from the date neatly inscribed on the cover sheet. That meant it had been in London in those limbo years after art school when I was lost and drifting. It was a time when my very *self* seemed to be something that might just melt away, that might just slip through my fingers, and so, I concluded, I had started to write it all down, as a way of fixing things. It must have been important to try to render something permanent, to shore it all up against an impending doom and to create roots into the past. But then, of course, things shifted again and I found a way forwards with my paintings, a wordless way of being in the world. I dealt instead with the currency of images, and all the papers, all the words, were packed away and forgotten.

Nonetheless, I had written it.

It was like looking at my own ghost. Or rather, reading a tale that had been written down by my own ghost. The narrator was both familiar and a stranger. It was a most peculiar sensation to read those words. Let me say it again, the events described did not correspond to the memories I had carried with me for so many years.

The tree was an after-image from a woozy dream, a ghostly presence. As I read the account, and reread it, I was struck by a growing sense of recognition. This crept up on me, as if I had read this story before somewhere.

After, having read it through several times with a building sense of both unease and familiarity, I wondered how I might reconcile the two versions of the story: the one in the manuscript and the one in my memory. Both might contain a truth.

Had I lost the tree in a kind of fugue? Perhaps it had been there all along, rooted deeply, growing upon me. Perhaps, unable to rationally explain what I had witnessed, I had processed it as a dream, or a kind of vision, and then furtively tucked it away in a shaded corner of my memory, retaining a more comfortable version of events; dreaming (or perhaps hoping) that the man had got up and walked away, never to be seen again?

If that was the case, I wondered, what else might I have lost? What else had fled? As I pondered this question, it seemed that my present life, my present *self*, was perhaps built upon profoundly unstable foundations, like one of the villages along the coast that would eventually succumb to the shifting lands and slip beneath the waves.

When I was younger I had been obsessed by tales of the

fantastic and implausible, fascinated by ghost stories and anything that evoked the possibility of a passage between this world
and some other. I had also been transfixed by the sheer weirdness of the natural world, which was part of the same mystery.
I was so gripped by the astonishing transformations of plants,
insects, moths and butterflies, the extraordinary intricacies of
fungal life, that I had eventually even made it the heart of my
professional life.

Nonetheless, the voice of the manuscript rang true. As I
absorbed the import of the words before me, it was coming
back. It swam unsteadily into uncertain focus, reminding me of
the way in which an image magically materialises on a sheet of
photographic paper in the bath of chemicals in the darkroom.
I saw then that the roots had gone deep, really gone deep.
Hidden, screened, buried, obscured, whatever you wanted to
call it, it had seeped through me and into everything I did, like
the ink from a pen forgotten in a jacket pocket, the stain over
the heart spreading like a dark flower unfolding.

Having read the manuscript, I saw again and anew the
reality of change. It was all around me, in every *thing*, and I
began to feel curiously weightless, as if I myself might shift
and transform at any moment (as of course I did, and as we
all do, from hour to hour and day to day and year to year).
Reading this strange tale, my eyes were finally opening to a
way of apprehending life and existence that I knew intuitively,
but which I had lost. I reflected that the great oak behind the
house in which I was then living presented a gaunt aspect
during the bleak winters, but would offer yellowy buds in the
spring, before bursting into leaf, reaching a luminous green that
heralded the arrival of the perfectly polished acorns and then

the slow spotting of the leaves with rust and then the curling and falling and finally, in winter, once again there would be just the bare branches, melancholy against a grey sky. In the garden beneath that tree I would watch the queer larvae in the undergrowth enter the pupa stage and then eventually emerge as magnificent butterfly or ominous moth. In the soil, the seed, sprouting, its tight case cracking open to reveal the first delicate frond. It was everywhere, ongoing.

It was everywhere. From that time I found that whenever I opened a book or watched a movie, transformation was there, in some form. Every story I read seemed to contain outlandish echoes of my own tale. The world began to feel unstable. Or, rather, the world began to feel as if it was in a permanent state of instability, or perhaps *becoming*. *Change is the natural state of things*, I thought. All objects – all organisms, all people and places – are in a state of unrest. Growth and decay. Entropy. These are the principles that underpin existence. We cannot resist this process of constant change, it is the law of the universe. We can only embrace it and be carried along on the flow.

Narcissus. Transformations into animals are relatively commonplace in Ovid's great poem. While transformations into vegetative beings are much rarer, there are a number scattered throughout. Alongside Daphne and Syrinx there are Philemon and Baucis, a devoted old couple who become oak and linden trees; Dryope, who picks a lotus in error and becomes a flower herself as a consequence; Cyparissus, who in grief for a fallen stag becomes a cypress tree; the grieving sisters of Phaethon, transformed into trees that weep amber; Leucothoe; Clytie;

the Maenads, Thracian women turned to trees by Bacchus; and the Apulian Shepherd, transformed into an olive tree. The most famous, however, is Narcissus.

It is likely you know the story. An exceptionally beautiful young man, vain and proud, spurning all the eager young women who fall for him, cruelly rejects the nymph Echo. In revenge, Nemesis causes him to fall in love with his own image, reflected in the water of a pool. Then, unable to tear himself away from the object of his devotion:

> *So melts the youth, and languishes away,*
> *His beauty withers, and his limbs decay . . .*

Time is compressed by these two simple lines. Are Ovid's transformations instantaneous or are they processes that play out over long minutes, patient hours or even days? The beauty of poetry, which causes images to be summoned by the imagination and held in the mind's eye, is that they can be both at the same time.

When the nymphs come to prepare Narcissus's body for burial, they find it has vanished. All that remains is the familiar flower, its tall rising stalk crowned by a luminous trumpet of bright yellow petals. So, this particular metamorphosis is doubly unusual in that it takes place *after* death.

It seems particularly appropriate that Narcissus's flower, the humble daffodil, is the harbinger of change, the augur of new life as spring follows the death of winter.

Inside. In a newspaper I read a story of a man in America who was admitted to hospital with severe chest pains. On examination it transpired he had a plant growing inside him. The doctor speculated that during a meal a pea had 'gone down the wrong way' – had been *inhaled* instead of ingested – and had become lodged in the lung, a warm and moist environment conducive to sprouting. At the time of admission it had grown to half an inch in length.

I think of Chloris in Botticelli's great painting, the incomparable *Primavera*, and the young shoots emerging from the nymph's open mouth. There is something sexual in it. Possession. Ecstasy. In that image, the transformation is beginning within. Unlike Bernini's Daphne, whose metamorphosis starts at her extremities, Botticelli's Chloris is evidently changing from the inside out.

Inevitably, I think of the way he coughed and how first seaweed and then thick clumps of leaves came up from somewhere deep within his body.

On another occasion I find a similar story in a popular tabloid newspaper. The story reports that a 'fir tree' has been found growing inside a man's lung by surgeons. The tree, which measured five centimetres in length, was discovered by doctors when they opened up the man to remove what they thought was a tumour.

As with the previous story, the doctors believed that the patient had inhaled a seed, which later sprouted inside his lung. The patient had complained of extreme pain in his chest and had been coughing up blood.

'We were a hundred per cent sure it was cancer,' said the surgeon. 'We did X-rays and found what looked exactly like a tumour. I had seen hundreds before, so we decided on surgery.' However, before removing a major part of the man's lung, as a precaution the surgeon investigated tissue taken in a biopsy.

'I thought I was hallucinating,' he said. 'I asked my assistant to have a look. I blinked three times as I was sure I was seeing things.'

The doctors believed the coughing of blood was caused by the tiny pine needles piercing blood capillaries. 'It was very painful. But to be honest I didn't feel a foreign object inside me,' the patient was quoted as saying.

Quadrats. It was a day I had been looking forward to. Mr Willing had designated it a day of experiments and 'field work'. We were to spend the morning in the classroom, taking it in turns to use our one and only Bunsen burner to heat test tubes of rare liquids, combining chemicals, measuring temperatures, and testing the acidity of various substances by dissolving them and then dripping droplets onto sheets of blotting paper and monitoring the rainbows of colour that crept slowly across the surface. In the afternoon, we were to venture out 'into the field'. As he said it, I had imagined an actual field, a verdant open space and Quill and I lying peacefully on our backs and making up names for the clouds drifting across the azure sky.

The morning passed without incident – no damaging spills, poisonings or burnings – and when we reconvened after lunch, we were split into pairs or small groups and Mr Willing gave us our assignment for the afternoon. We were to perform something called quadrat surveys. Mr Willing handed out the quadrats, white-painted wooden frames about three feet by three feet square, and explained the methodology.

'The idea here,' he said, 'is to look at species density and distribution within a given habitat. We're assessing what grows where, and how much of it. Now, if we want to know how many grasses there are in any given habitat area, how would we go about that?'

Marjorie Eager put her hand up.

'Yes, Marge?'

'Count them,' she said, pleased with herself.

'Exactly, it's obvious, isn't it?' said Mr Willing. 'But if we want to know, for example, how many specimens of a particular kind of grass there are on our marshes, what is the problem with your method?'

Silence.

'I'll tell you. You can't go out and count every single blade of grass in the marshes, can you? Impossible. Where would you draw the line? Where does the marsh end, exactly?'

He paused.

'So, what we do is take some random samples using our quadrats' – he held one up so that it framed him, as if he were a child pretending to be a newscaster on the television – 'counting the number of any particular species within each. And then, if we know the total area we are investigating, we can do some simple calculations and deduce the approximate number of specimens within it. If our quadrat is, say, one square foot and we're surveying an area one hundred feet by ten feet we multiply our findings by a thousand and we then have an average. Now, the number will be approximate, but it will give us a clear idea of population, density and so on. Understood?'

We all nodded. Scratching of pencils in exercise books.

'Good. Now, the samples must be random, otherwise a fool

like Marsh here might deliberately select samples containing an abundance of a particular species and so skew the calculations.' Sidney Marsh, a sleepy child with pronounced freckles who made a habit of coming bottom of the class, grinned and gave Mr Willing a thumbs up. 'If we were doing this rigorously, scientifically, we would use a method for randomising your selections – by dividing our sample area into a grid and allowing you all to draw grid numbers from a hat, for example – but we're not going to bother with that. Today we're more interested in exploring how the environment – its botanical composition, to be precise – changes as the landscape changes. So, you're going to begin at the shore. Yes, out on the shingle. And then I want you to take samples on the marsh, in the woods and then finally up on the heath. You'll all do one survey in each location and then when we collate all the information we'll have enough to come up with some conclusions about biodiversity, cause and effect, and so on. We can think about why certain plants grow closer to the sea than others, or why some like the woods and others don't, and ask if the woods or the shore are more fertile and diverse. Then you'll write those conclusions up. That'll be your homework.'

He handed out the quadrats and some old field guides from the school library, so that we might identify the various grasses, flowers and suchlike we were likely to encounter.

'Sir,' said Quill. 'What if we can't identify something?'

'In that unlikely event, I suggest you make a detailed draw-ing, with notes, and then perhaps we'll be able to come up with an identification back here in the classroom. OK?'

We gathered our things together.

'I want you back here by four,' he said. 'Also, while our aim is to survey the flora of this slice of our land, we must not forget the fauna. If you find you have a critter or critters within your quadrat then record them too.'

'Critters, sir?' asked Quill.

'Yes, bugs, insects, worms, creepy crawlies, small mammals ...'

'Marsh,' he said, as we traipsed out, 'Marsh, when you are in the marsh, try not to throw your quadrat into the marsh. And don't fall in the marsh, Marsh.'

Mr Willing chuckled at his own wit and a gentle ripple of hilarity passed through the room. Sidney rolled his eyes and groaned good naturedly. The prospect of an afternoon 'in the field' instead of in the classroom meant that everyone was in good spirits. 'Seriously though,' said Mr Willing, 'please don't throw your quadrats into the water. Neither sea nor pond. Someone will have to retrieve it and you can be sure it won't be me. Right, off you go. I'll follow on and check on your progress in a bit.'

The sun was shining. We ambled down the road from the school and crossed the coast road onto the marsh track, quickly forming into little groups. Sidney soon fell behind, wandering along in his own world. *I could be like that*, I thought to myself: solitary, disconnected. As an only child it was a natural state. But today I was enjoying the company of my classmates.

Quill walked ahead, chatting to Bill Castle, and I watched her. Tall, wiry, with her fine sharp white teeth and long fingers, her hair an uncontrollable mass of dark brown curls, burnished bronze in sunlight, coiled and alive so that she looked like a Medusa. The ease of her movements. Every now and again she glanced back at me. I stuck my tongue out at her.

120

I felt a simple happiness, walking out across the marsh like that, with an intriguing task at hand, the sun warming my skin. When we reached the shingle bank Quill and I split off from the others and walked down the shoreline a way until we found a good spot to sit. The sea was calm and quiet, an unbroken plane of pale grey bisecting the universe. We sat in silence gazing out into the emptiness. Looking back, I saw that some of the others were doing the same, and that Bill was smoking a cigarette, slow smoke blue in the sunshine. Mr Willing was nowhere to be seen and I imagined him still in the classroom, his feet up on his desk, reading a novel. Our fieldwork would be as welcome to him as it was to us.

'Come on,' said Quill, 'let's get this done.'

She stood and with a smooth nimble movement flung the quadrat over her head so that it spun through the air and landed above and behind us on the shingle bank.

We scrambled up, the stones shifting and crunching beneath our feet releasing the ripe crabby aromas of the shore, and knelt beside the small white square.

'Nope, nothing here,' I said. The quadrat neatly framed a simple composition of brown and grey pebbles, some pieces of flint and a single smoothed shard of green sea glass. Some shells. A leftover of glistening seaweed.

'Do we record that?' asked Quill, pointing at the rubbery sea scrap.

'Nope,' I said. I tossed it further down the beach.

Quill grinned at me, showing her small even teeth. We opened our notebooks and each carefully drew a square divided into nine smaller squares. I labelled mine: *Quadrat Surveys. 1. The Shore.*

But there was nothing to add, so we left them blank and then moved on.

We trailed back across the marsh, arm in arm, but halfway in cut off on a faint path that went left, running parallel to the shoreline. Some of our classmates were also making their way back from the sea edge, and we could see Mr Willing, now striding purposefully down the path from the road.

In a small scrape a stone's throw from the main path I tossed the quadrat into a patch of grasses edging a drift of reeds. 'That'll do,' I said, and Quill and I hunkered down and began our survey.

Mr Willing waved at us as he followed the main path down towards the shingle.

Grass, sedge, sea lavender, spearwort. One small beetle: species unknown.

We regained the path and a group of us walked together up through the village and into the woods.

In the woods Quill and I chose a clearing beneath an old oak tree. Quill turned her back to the tree and again tossed the quadrat over her shoulder. It landed among some leaf litter. While the only plant we could see was a tiny oak seedling, the leaf mould was teeming with woodlice, earwigs and a frenzied centipede. We counted them as best we could and made a note in our books. Given the lack of flora we decided to take another sample and I threw the quadrat across the clearing into the undergrowth. Here we found ferns, wood sorrel, dead nettles, ivy and an exhausted foxglove, its flower spike browned and broken.

After, we followed the path up on to the heath. Some of our classmates were already coming back down, having completed the task. Others were still behind us.

Following the path between stands of furzy gorse and mounds of heather, we looked for a suitable sample site. Away from the path the low-lying growth was tangled, and Quill simply dropped the quadrat at her feet. Here, pushing aside the grasses that filled the square we found something unusual. At first, I was shocked, vaguely repulsed, thinking we had unwittingly revealed a wounded animal, or some hairless infant creature, but then we saw that it was a plant.

'An orchid?' wondered Quill and took the field guide out.

It was small, with dark green leaves covered in fine hairs, and on a stumpy stem it bore a flower that looked strangely like a mouth, pink and white with curious veins of purple and shots of yellow along the edges of the petal.

We looked it up in the field guide but couldn't find it. Once we looked closer, we could see that it didn't conform to any of the types of plant listed, even the orchids.

What was it? It was brazenly erotic, horribly sensual. The real word for it was *lascivious*. Labial, priapic, swollen, moist, weirdly inviting. Unidentifiable. We examined it through a magnifying glass that Quill had brought, and she wanted to put her finger inside it.

'Please don't,' I said. 'In case it's poisonous.'

I turned the page in my notebook and started to make a careful drawing of it.

We became conscious of Mr Willing talking to another group a short distance away and Quill called to him.

'Sir, look at this,' she said, as he came over. 'It's something odd and we can't find it in the book.'

Mr Willing crouched and pulled back the grasses to reveal it.

'Well, that is unusual,' he said. 'I've never seen anything like that before.'

He too flicked through the pages of the field guide but soon gave up.

'Shall we dig it up and take it back to the classroom?'

'No, I'll make a note and come back later and have a proper look.' He took a handkerchief from his jacket pocket and tied it around a nearby beech sapling. 'Just mark it down on your survey as species unknown.' I finished my drawing and made some colour notes in the margin, as I didn't have any paints or coloured pencils with me.

Quill considered the drawing, which I now suppose was my first real work of botanical art. 'That's rather good, you know,' she said, smiling. 'Even if it does look like a fanny.'

I laughed at that, but I wasn't sure if I should be pleased or not.

Some time later, towards the end of that same term, I was late with some homework and went to hand it in to Mr Willing after classes had finished. In a friendly manner he asked how my studies were progressing and complimented me on my drawings.

'Sir,' I asked, 'did you ever work out what that flower was?'

He hadn't. He had been unable to find it in any of his reference books. He had been back to have another look and had thought to take some photographs but for whatever reason had not got round to it. A week or so later he had passed the site again and hadn't been able to find a trace of it.

'You know,' he said, thoughtfully, 'it's possible it was a discovery, something new. A completely new species. As its finder, we might have named it after you. How about that? But more likely it was an anomaly, a one-off mutation or hybrid coming from one of the common orchids. I don't suppose we'll ever know now. Just goes to show how much there is – even here on our doorstep – that we don't understand.'

Hallucinations. Recently, as I have been trying to understand the implications of what I committed to paper all those years ago, my thoughts have been circling around the great and strange paintings of Bosch. We don't know a great deal about Jheronimus van Aken, who took as his professional moniker the name of his home town, 's-Hertogenbosch, usually referred to as Den Bosch, the 'wood' or 'forest'. I have been reading about him and looking at his work, for in the paintings of 'Hieronymus of the Wood', there are several striking representations of human-plant hybridity and metamorphosis.

Leafing through a yellowed volume entitled *Masterpieces of the Northern Renaissance* I came across a double page spread of the famous *Garden of Earthly Delights*, in the collection of the Prado in Madrid. That unprecedented triptych may or may not tell the story of mankind via two side panels representing Paradise or the Garden of Eden, and hell, and a central panel representing either an imaginary world in which the Fall did not come to pass, or an allegory of unchastity and moral decline. Fascinated by this extraordinary picture, which I had known before but which I had never really looked at in detail, I decided to find out more about Bosch's world and bought a monograph. There I discovered the paintings known as *The Haywain* and *The Temptation of Saint Anthony*, among many others.

There are two versions of *The Haywain* and it is apparently possible that neither is by Bosch himself but rather they are later copies of a lost original. Nonetheless, we can be sure that the composition is Bosch's own graphic invention; the visual language deployed is distinctly and uniquely his own. As in the *Garden of Earthly Delights*, the two side panels of the triptych depict Paradise and hell. The central panel depicts a huge hay wagon surrounded by an astonishing array of figures engaged in a bizarre range of activities; some are dancing, some are fighting. A man lies on the ground as his throat is slit by another who sits astride him. The cart is at the centre of a great procession, drawn on towards hell by an assembly of grotesque demons and followed after by a mass of people, including even the Emperor and the Pope. Before the cart, the last demon pulling the vehicle onwards is a grey figure in a blue cowl, with a thin face. I study him closely. His left leg is a tree trunk, rooted into the earth or, rather, he emerges from the trunk, as if the bark gaped open and he slithered out. Branches sprout from his shoulders and he grips them with his own hand, as if trying to restrain his own ongoing transformation.

The Temptation of Saint Anthony is another triptych and shows the travails of the saint, beset and tormented by bizarre visions. In the left panel we see him carried up into the sky by demons and then dropped to the ground. Below him a figure on all fours becomes part of the landscape and branches sprout from his naked legs into a sort of rocky outcrop. In the right-hand panel, the saint sits in a landscape, consulting a book, and a naked woman emerges from a hollow tree to tempt him. In the central panel the saint, remarkably serene given his circumstances, is at the very centre of a hellish maelstrom of activity. Amid burning and ruined buildings thronged with bizarre animals, monsters and demons, another procession of figures extends. To the left, monsters enter, led by a man who appears to be wearing a headpiece made from a hollow tree. To the right, a pale white figure rides a giant rat and cradles what may be either a corpse or a swaddled child. His body tapers to a narrow reptilian tail but his head and shoulders become a mass of knotted wood and branches, seemingly dead and lifeless. His thin blue face looks out from a broken cavity in the wood and I wonder if he might even be the same abject creature who draws the great hay cart on to hell.

In the centre of the painting there is a weird detail: a severed foot lies on a piece of white cloth. This, I read, is almost certainly a reference to ergotism, the condition known as 'hellfire' or 'Saint Anthony's Fire', which in Bosch's time was an epidemic. It was caused by a fungus called ergot which grows upon rye grains. The grains were baked into bread and then eaten. Depending on the specific ergot alkaloids involved it caused either a horrible tissue death – in which limbs ultimately turned black and fell off, accompanied by terrible burning pains – or seizures, mania and hallucinations. Ingestion of this fungus thus caused victims to see visions such as those experienced by the saint in Bosch's painting. Hundreds of years after Bosch died, a man named Albert Hofmann made LSD from an alkaloid called ergotamine found in the fungus.

Thinking about Bosch's oeuvre, however, it is the figure known as the Tree Man, the unprecedented figure who stands at the centre of his vision of hell in the *Garden of Earthly Delights*, to whom I am irresistibly drawn back again and again with horrified compulsion. He haunts me. His flesh has the same awful colourlessness as the tree-demon, and reminds me of the fish-white paleness of the man on the beach. Looking at him, I know his skin will be cold and hard to touch. His body is shaped like an egg but is cracked and open at the rear. Inside, a group of naked people sit at a table, while a maid draws beer from a barrel. One uses a toad as a seat. The Tree Man's legs, which sprout long sharp-looking growths that pierce his own body in an unnerving act of auto-penetration, are set in two boats, suggesting extreme instability. Above his head a broad white disc, like the wide brim of a hat, supports parading pairs of sinners and demons and a huge pink sac that may be a kind of bagpipe. Below the brim, he looks back over his shoulder at us, with an expression of amusement.

It has been suggested that this a self-portrait.

What it all means no one can say with any certainty.

The strange gifts of the sea. Many odd things are washed up on the shore. There are natural wonders such as flints shaped like fingers, the black egg sacs known as *mermaid's purses*, cuttlefish bones, and the pieces of wood so worn by the water that they have taken on extraordinary new forms and resemble corals or Modernist sculptures. There are old ordnances, ancient tools, bits of farm machinery, bottles containing faded and illegible messages, the remains of wrecks and just about every other thing we can imagine.

In recent years, I have read, visitors to the beaches of the Salish Sea, around Seattle and Vancouver, have sometimes found severed human feet washed up there.

Hallucinations. As I began to think about the transformative powers of certain plants, I became fixated upon the notion that the metamorphosis, if it happened at all, had been caused or enabled by something he had ingested: a plant or drug, or both. I theorised that he had taken something and it had 'rooted' inside him and changed his body from the inside out.

I was intrigued by the notion that certain plant extracts might effect psychic and even physiological change. I thought of the everyday pick-me-ups, tea, coffee and tobacco, the soporific calmness induced by lavender and valerian. I had smoked cannabis at art school and found it not so much transformative as entropic. Far from opening up glistening new vistas of consciousness or recasting reality in a brilliant new light, it just made me foggy and sluggish and confused. My thoughts became leaden and my body weary. It was disappointing and so, after a few trials, I didn't explore its effects any further.

But after art school, at that time when I was somewhat lost and unsure of which direction to follow in my life, I conducted my first and only psychedelic experiment, and experienced an inkling of what might be called plant (or *fungal*) consciousness (or, perhaps more accurately, what academics call 'non-animal consciousness'). Without access to peyote, salvia or ayahuasca, my investigation was limited to indigenous hallucinogens. Now, as I reflect upon those curious events, this experience seems to be connected in an obscure way to the events of *The North Shore*, as so many things are.

I had a job for the summer with an outdoor pursuits centre on the border with Wales. Despite my essentially solitary nature, I enjoyed working with the children and helping the instructors who taught sailing, canoeing, pony trekking and hiking. We all lived under canvas, each in our own small tent, and ate communally in a mess hall. I remember it as a time of freedom.

In conversation with some of the older instructors I discovered that so-called magic mushrooms grew abundantly on the playing field we used for archery lessons. There had been much rain that summer and the mushrooms were so plentiful and of such apparently unprecedented size that Higgs, a particularly devoted enthusiast who resembled a Viking, had taken the extreme measure of installing a 'drying cabinet' in his tent. It was a large wooden chest acquired from a local charity shop, with multiple newspaper-lined drawers, and was so large that there was no room for a bed. Higgs therefore slept out in the field, among the mushrooms. Through making regular harvests he hoped to lay in enough supplies for a year, even more.

I resolved to explore the effects of psilocybin but, being still somewhat shy, I decided to do it on my own. This was perhaps foolhardy.

I asked Higgs to show me how to identify the correct mushrooms and advise on what to do with them, saying I was just curious. He was an enormous man, with long curly blond hair that fell around his shoulders and a permanent smile. He laughed and winked at me. One Saturday afternoon, having picked a handful of the weird little fruitbodies Higgs directed me towards, I retired to my tent hoping to explore a new inner world. I brewed tea on my tiny camping stove, letting the tangle of fungal grey steep with the leaves. The resulting brown brew was truly revolting and so I sweetened it with honey, as Higgs had advised. I filled a cup and, thinking to exercise care, took a few mouthfuls and settled back to see what happened. It was a fine sunny day, and I remember lying back on my makeshift bed made from pallets and looking out through the open door of the tent to see the trees waving with the breeze and clouds washing across the blue sky. Motes of dust were caught in shafts of oblique sunlight, dancing lazily in space. Remote galaxies. Atoms. I was aware of the background noise of the camp: a medley of voices, a game of football being played somewhere nearby.

I waited. Nothing happened.

I drank some more and tried to read a book but found that I couldn't concentrate.

After some time, I decided to go for a walk. I left the camp and followed one of the tracks that led up into the hills. All the while I was acutely self-conscious, monitoring myself for any sensation that was out of the ordinary, waiting for the onset of the visions, or whatever it would be. Perhaps due to the rigorous self-analysis I was subjecting myself to, I had the profound sensation that I was apart from myself: two selves, one interiorised and the other externalised, the latter hovering over my body and watching the former as it picked its way up the stony path. I noticed that the leaves on the trees were extremely green, but perhaps that was just the light. Or was it that my sense of vision was somehow enhanced? It was hard to tell. The birds were singing and there were insects buzzing, flying, crawling and burrowing: an intensity of feverish activity of which I was acutely aware.

As I walked back down to the camp I concluded that something was different after all, but that it wasn't clear to me what it was. The nervousness had dissipated and I felt fine, if a little unusual. I realised I was stepping very lightly, as if I had become weightless. I began to have the agreeable sensation that

I was floating just above the ground, just by a fraction of an inch, no more.

At my tent I drank some more of the revolting tea and lay down again. Time passed. It was now early evening and my experiment was proving somewhat underwhelming. I decided that the mushrooms I had picked must have been a weaker strain, or that my preparation had been faulty. Nothing was really happening. I resolved to walk to the village and go to The Red Lion, the local pub where all the staff would congregate in the evenings at weekends. That was when it started.

Stumbling down the hollow lane that led to the village I was aware not only that I was unsteady but that the trees that arched over above me were waving and leaning in and trying to touch me. It was not an aggressive or intimidating sensation but rather a gesture of kinship. Something in me, a new quality I had not previously been aware of, reached out to them too, although no physical contact was made.

I stopped and looked around me. Everything glittered with detail and clarity, an impossibly complex matrix of being and coming-into-being. The sky had become iridescent, made of oily light refracted through an enormous crystal.

In The Red Lion it was busy and everything was so much more vivid than usual: louder, brighter, more colourful. Quite a few of my colleagues were there, massed around several tables, talking loudly and playing pool. Higgs spotted me and came over, grinning broadly. His golden hair was like a bright halo ringing his happy face. He seemed to glow.

'All right?' he asked, winking again. He peered at me.

I nodded and smiled. I was happy, it was true. But speech was a problem.

Higgs laughed and went back to the pool table. Ordering a drink was an extreme exercise in muscle control. I sat on a wooden bench close to the door with a pint, pretending to read a paperback. I felt everyone was watching me; familiar and unfamiliar faces winked and smiled and laughed if I looked up from my book. Everyone *knew*. But what did they know? I was warm and relaxed – but also disorientated. The lights in the pub were becoming kaleidoscopic. The sounds were orchestral. As the effects became more noticeable everything began to emit an aura of coloured light, even people and inanimate objects. Soft flashes and sunspots kept on bursting silently across my field of vision: coronas of iridescent light, azure, vermilion, cadmium, sunflower yellow, violet, iris blue. I was unable to follow any conversation, the noises compressed inside the busy room merging together and becoming a symphonic babble.

Then I became supremely aware of the various textures of things: the hardness of the wooden bar, the giving plushness of the seat I sat on, the paperiness of the cardboard beer mat, the wetness of the beer and the strange way it sparkled and fizzed in my mouth and on my tongue, which felt like it had expanded and become a new and extraordinary organ, one with no confirmed purpose but which prevented the possibility of speech.

I began to feel *mushroomy*. By which I mean soft and fibrous, as if my skeleton had dissolved within me, leaving only an undifferentiated matrix of spongy tissue. Yes, the density of my body was changing. Hard bone and muscle were becoming something soft, a foamy fleshiness of a ripe fungal fruitbody, worked through with a neural network consisting of a million microscopic mycelial tendrils. Sitting on the wooden bench I wondered if I might begin to subtly infiltrate its physical matter if I stayed still long enough. I pushed at my arms and legs with my fingers as if to test the firmness of my own body, rubbed my eyes and ears, and drank some more beer.

I had surely only been in the pub for a few minutes, but it was getting dark when I stumbled out into the peace and stillness. The lane back to the camp was now like a dark tunnel through a purely vegetal universe. I was surrounded by a swaying, teeming atmosphere of vegetation, a countless assembly of individual organisms, from bacteria and bugs in the soil all the way up to the great oaks that roofed the road, and which had formed into a single totality of unified consciousness. Of which I felt, extraordinarily, that I was a part. The wind was blowing through me, as through the canopy of the trees. What did I feel in the tips of my fingers, my ears and nose? That I was changing somehow?

I had become plant-like, interconnected, a network, wholly botanical. Could I communicate? I could, in that moment. But what could I say? It didn't matter. It would be said. It was being said. It would be understood.

My reverie was broken as I heard people coming up the lane behind me, talking noisily, Higgs among them, and so I crept through an opening in the hedge into a meadow with long grass where I lay down. I enjoyed the hardness of the earth at my back and looked up into the sky, trying to absorb this extraordinary sensation of connectedness. Feeling that my physical being might simply dissolve and be dispersed among this wonderful organic labyrinth.

After a while I got up and stumbled my way back to the camp, now quiet and enclosed in darkness. Outside my tent I vomited, copiously.

I lay on my bed and it took a very long time to go to sleep because of the teeming and infinite universe out there beyond the canvas, the flowing energy.

This is the closest I have come to the feeling of *becoming* plant. I still wonder if *he* felt something like that. That uncanny connection, both belonging and becoming.

The next day there was a lingering sensation of something, but what it was I couldn't quite put my finger on.

The Thing from Another World, 1951. These days my nights are often solitary and that is my preference. While I do sometimes enjoy company I find the few social interactions my work entails, as pleasant as they are, exhaust and distract me. The work is intensely demanding of hand and eye. So, in the evenings I usually read or watch old movies.

This one is in black and white. Something has crashed into the ice near a remote American base in the Antarctic. A team flies out to the crash site to investigate and as they spread out to determine the shape of the object beneath the ice, they realise they are standing in a wide circle. It is a flying saucer. As the men attempt to melt the ice to reach it they inadvertently trigger a chain reaction with the craft's metal alloy hull, resulting in a massive explosion. The vessel is completely destroyed. However, a Geiger counter detects something, a body, buried nearby. They excavate it in a large block of ice, load it aboard the plane and then fly out just as a terrible storm closes in.

Back at the base, the block of ice is secured in a storeroom and the men set a watch. In the night, the block thaws and whatever was encased within breaks out. As it attempts to escape the base, it is attacked by the sled dogs before stumbling off into the storm. When the men reach the scene they find that two of the dogs have been killed. But they have somehow severed the creature's arm.

In the lab, the scientists examine the arm, and come to the astonishing conclusion that the alien is an advanced form of plant life. Cutting it open, they find seed pods inside. There is a moment of comedy when Skeely, an opportunistic journalist looking for a story, sceptically suggests the creature is a kind of 'super carrot'. But the chief scientist, Carrington, rebuffs him by pointing out that it is in fact 'a carrot that can construct a ship beyond our terrestrial intelligence, of materials we have not yet created – and guide it through sixty million miles or more of space.'

He goes on to explain that there is already knowledge of plants on earth that demonstrate processes akin to thought, such as the telegraph vine and the acanthus century plant. 'There are hundreds of other examples,' he says. 'No, Mr Skeely, intelligence in vegetables and plants is an old story on this planet of ours. Older even than the animal arrogance that has overlooked it.'

The men look on in horror as the hand comes alive, flexing its fingers, and Carrington speculates that it is a carnivorous being, revived by the blood of the dead sled dogs.

Carrington's admiration for the alien creature is undisguised. He and his colleague Chapman discuss its 'neat and uncon-fused' reproductive processes, akin to those of plants. 'No pain or pleasure as we know them,' says Chapman. 'No heart.' 'None,' says Carrington. 'Our superior in every way.'

After this moment of high weirdness, the movie defaults to

more conventional genre expectations. The 'monster', when it finally appears, is frankly a let-down. It is obviously just a man in a suit and is, dramatically speaking, a disappointment after the tense build-up. I'm honestly expecting something way more out there to reward my patient vigil in front of my TV so late into the night. Tentacles, foliage, and so on. Nonetheless, there is another striking scene, where it is revealed that Carrington, obsessed with the alien, has initiated a very strange experiment. Using seeds taken from the severed arm, he has confirmed his hypothesis that the creature is carnivorous and needs blood to live, and has been growing small alien plants by feeding them from the blood plasma supply kept at the base. 'Human plants!' exclaims one of the scientists in astonishment. The small plants pulse and throb with horrible vitality.

The alien is finally destroyed – incinerated by electricity – and Skeely has his moment of glory, broadcasting the story, beginning with that famous warning: 'Tell the world. Tell this to everybody, wherever they are. Watch the skies everywhere. Keep looking. Keep watching the skies.'

The Quatermass Xperiment, 1955. It is late again. A winter's night, cold and dark. I have a good bottle of red for company after a long day at the studio. I turn on the TV and there's another old black-and-white movie. An astronaut has returned to earth, but something has gone terribly wrong. It seems generic and at first I don't pay much attention, but slowly I am drawn in, as I always am.

The very first manned space flight has crash-landed some-where in the English Home Counties. A lone figure, the only survivor of a crew of three, staggers from the crashed rocket and falls to the ground.

In the laboratory it becomes clear that something inexplicable has happened during the flight. The astronaut, Caroon, is almost catatonic. He cannot speak, but his gaunt face and haunted eyes convey both pain and distress.

His wife visits with a bunch of roses and when she pricks her finger on one of the thorns and bleeds a little he stirs for the first time. The doctor examining him points to his shoulder, which appears to be swollen and disfigured, and then suggests that something is happening to the bone structure of his face: 'There's been a change ...' he says, ominously. His superior, the scientist in charge of the so-called 'experimental rocket programme', is a brusque American. He shouts a lot and is weirdly out of place among all the terribly polite Brits. The police take fingerprints from Caroon. They are degraded and on examining them the American proclaims: 'But these prints aren't even ... human!' It is great melodrama. I'm hooked.

Later Caroon rises from his bed and reaches out for the roses, now in a vase, before collapsing. Later still he escapes from the hospital, but not before the presence of a potted cactus causes him to react in distress. He smashes it with his bare hand, embedding broken spines in his flesh.

Meanwhile, the scientist speculates that in space an alien organism infiltrated the rocket and fused with the astronaut, producing a 'union between plant and animal ...' He goes on to explain, dramatically, 'Of course, like any living thing ... to live ... it must have food!'

Next we see Caroon enter a pharmacy and search desperately through the assorted bottles. When interrupted by a pharmacist he reacts violently, killing him by clubbing him with his arm, which is now grotesquely swollen but also scarred and sprouting vicious cactus thorns. The film is black and white, but you know, watching it, that the flesh has become discoloured and is undoubtedly a sickly vegetative green. When the police arrive they speculate he has stolen certain chemicals to try to accelerate the transformation overtaking him. Not to stop it, but to *accelerate* it. They find the body of the pharmacist, now just a hollow husk, sucked dry.

The next morning, having spent the night hiding on a river barge, Caroon encounters a little girl. He keeps his mutating arm hidden by his coat but in her innocence, she is not afraid of him despite his increasingly eccentric behaviour and appearance. Echoes of James Whale's wonderful *Frankenstein*, I think, filling my glass again.

It's the last we see of the astronaut. Increasingly the police are tracking a trail of slime. The astronaut's terrible metamorphosis embodies a sense of physical fragility, as the boundaries of the human body become increasingly porous and then indeterminate.

When the authorities finally catch up with the creature, almost no trace of its human host is left; it is an enormous squirming mass of tissue: part plant, part fungus, part tentacular sea creature: a deep-sea (space) monster adrift in the Gothic coral reef that is Westminster Abbey. Again, it is electricity, with all its progressive connotations of modernity, that is the weapon that destroys the alien threat. The American electrocutes it, diverting all of London's power into the creature, and it bursts into flames before it can release its deadly spores.

*

The fire. The children – for to be honest, we were still children then – had gathered on the beach. It was Quill's birthday. For her celebration she chose a site on the marsh side of the shingle banks, half a mile or so along the coast from the village, where there was protection from the onshore winds. That morning, with a couple of friends, we had combed the beach for driftwood and built a pyre.

In the evening, I arrived late, just in time for the lighting of the fire. I can't now remember why that was, but I think there may have been some reluctance on my part to go at all. I didn't like to share Quill with the others. It was already dusk when I set off across the marsh track, a bottle of cider heavy in my shoulder bag. A V of geese went overhead, high up, and everything felt auspicious.

As the sun set, dipping into the heath and washing the sky with mauve and violet, Quill ceremoniously put a light to the pile of wood. The flames leapt up and the whole scene immediately took on a witchy aspect. The air quickly cooled as darkness slid over us and everyone gathered close to the fire for warmth. Some had blankets they wrapped around themselves. It was quite a gathering, almost everyone from our class and even some of the older kids. Bill Castle had a guitar and started to play folk songs, his voice high and pure. Some sang along and others beat an unruly percussion on a rusty barrel or against blocks of wood scavenged from the shoreline. Someone had a harmonica and played a rough blues to Bill's rudimentary twelve-bar accompaniment. Bottles of beer and cider were passed around, flickering gold in the flamelight. The blue smoke of hand-rolled cigarettes combined with the white smoke of the fire eddying and billowing this way and that as the wind dropped and turned.

Soon the marshes were shrouded and the night shrank to the pool of light cast by the fire, and there at the centre of it was Quill, her face painted by flames, a pagan priestess, leading the dance.

Chatter. Drinking. Too many conversations running together and overlapping to follow them all. We competed to identify the constellations drifting above us in a clear night sky. Someone spotted a slow-moving star, a satellite most likely, tracing an invisible border between our atmosphere and outer space. Bill started playing and singing 'Little Red Rooster' and we sang along as the percussion started up again.

Flirtations. Awakenings. Hormones racing through us, transformative.

The moon rose.

In a lull I found myself seated next to Bill, who was absently picking a three-note arpeggio over and over. He leant over. *Help me with this*, he said, *I'm doing a poll. Lennon or McCartney?*

Neither, thanks, I replied. I dared not tell him that we didn't listen to pop music in our house.

He looked at me like I'd lost my mind and started strumming 'She Loves You'.

Later, when some had headed home, keeping to their curfews, and some had drunkenly fallen asleep under blankets by the fire, the rest, including Quill, climbed the shingle and stumbled down to the water's edge where they stripped to their underwear and waded out into the cold sea. I followed, fearful, but drawn onwards. Moonlight bounced and scattered about their pale bodies like a silver fire. I watched from the top of the shingle, conflicted, and then returned to the warmth of the bonfire. I could not join them. The flames were dying down by then and the cold was creeping closer, and so I gathered up my things and without saying goodbye to anyone, even Quill, made my way back across the marsh. My head was throbbing from the cider and my mouth tasted of bitter tobacco. As I breathed deep of the cold clean air, a kind of clarity returned. The marsh in the night was beautiful. Distant galaxies wheeled above. Shooting stars. The call of an owl was a kind of blessing.

It is hard to be so much on the edge of things.

There would be many other such nights out on the shore, with fire and music. Among the dunes that edge the pine woods to the north, where a wide sweep of sand forms a plane bisecting sea and sky and where sandy dips and hollows with their crenulations of marram grass and broken fence posts offer privacy: places for secrets. But that night on the shingle is the one I remember clearest. We had tapped into something primal, some current that runs through the earth, and drawn it up out of the land, using a feral kind of magic.

***Invasion of the Body Snatchers*, 1956.** Prompted by my explorations – I hesitate to call it 'research' – I seek this one out. It's a classic. A doctor encounters a series of patients apparently suffering from Capgras delusion, the belief that one's relatives have been replaced with physically identical impostors. Initially, he thinks he is witnessing an outbreak of hysteria, but gradually comes to realise that something far more sinister is happening. That evening, the doctor's friend discovers – in his own home – a body with his own exact physical features, but indistinct, half-formed, as though not fully developed. Later, more duplicates are discovered, emerging from giant seed pods in the doctor's greenhouse. It becomes apparent that the entire population of the town is being systematically replaced with doubles while they sleep.

Alien spores have fallen from space and grown into large seed pods. Each one is capable of reproducing an exact duplicate of a human being. As each pod reaches full development, it assimilates the physical characteristics, memories and personality of a sleeping person placed near it. However, the copies are devoid of all human emotion.

After the film I find myself reflecting on what I have just seen. Like *The Thing from Another World*, *The Quatermass Xperiment* and many others, *Invasion of the Body Snatchers* is a story of its time, of the Cold War and fears of invasion. But it also speaks of a different kind of invasion, of disease and bodily transformation. Perhaps too it embodies a more profound terror, a fear of the loss of individual identity, of being subsumed into a larger whole.

But there is something else too. Why is it, I ask myself, that in these movies the source of the terror – the monster – is a form of plant life? It must be something about the *otherness* of plants, their inherent strangeness, that allows them to play this particular dramatic role. Plants are everywhere but most of us don't really pay attention to them. They exist in the background, as a backdrop. We ignore them, such is their ubiquity. But when we do turn our gaze upon the plant world, and look closely, what do we see? There is perverse eroticism in the grotesque sexual display of flowers, there is a disturbing carnality in the ways they feed on dead and dying matter, and we see an uncanny vitality, a sense of unruly and uncontrollable growth that might potentially overwhelm everything.

They are everywhere, and thriving. If an alien being landed on earth and conducted a survey of life, they would almost certainly conclude that plants, not animals (and certainly not humans), are the dominant life form.

Plants have no moral dimension. They just are. As Carrington says, they have no 'heart'. Their existence is devoted to the simple imperative to survive and perpetuate the species. This single-minded – and single-*minded* is an odd figure of speech in this context – focus, is, seen from a particular anthropocentric perspective, simply terrifying.

I remember well the paranoia of the Cold War, and also the excitement of the space race and the spectacle of the moon landing in 1969, watched on a fuzzy black-and-white television set Father purchased especially for the occasion. I've also wondered if witnessing men walking on the moon for the very first time cracked something inside him, for he left us not long after. That takes me back to the coming of the man from the sea. His arrival on our shore was as alien and inexplicable as if he were a stranger from another planet. After watching such movies, it does occur to me that he may indeed have come from another world.

Later that night I have an exceptionally vivid dream in which all the wooden objects in my bedroom, including the bed frame on which I lie sleeping, the chair and the wardrobe, become animated, alive. Green shoots begin to sprout from them with unnerving quickness, becoming woody and filling the space, like Struwwelpeter's fingernails. And then the wooden floorboards themselves begin to writhe and pulse with unruly energy, and shoots spring up, thickening quickly into knotty branches and rising. As the room fills with a tangle of probing tendrils and budded fronds they penetrate and pass through me as if I am insubstantial, a ghost in my own body. I am Bosch's Tree Man. The dream ends when the room has become completely choked with dark growth, an utterly entangled and chaotic thicket, and I cannot move, threaded and tied.

The Oak Tree. *Sir Robert Bennington of Brilliant Hall was visited by Elizabeth I during her state journey through the county in 1578. He made her many elaborate gifts and was rewarded with the title of High Constable. Shortly afterwards he threw a great banquet to celebrate, gathering friends and associates together from across the land. Although he was not well liked, and indeed had wronged many men in his life, such was his power and influence at that time that none could decline his invitation.*

As the guests gathered in the great hall a stranger stepped forward, bowed before Sir Robert, and said in an unfamiliar accent, My Lord, I should like to show you a marvel. Sir Robert nodded his assent and the stranger pulled from his pocket an acorn and held it up for all to see. Some of the guests drew close to inspect it and some handled it to test its weight and passed it from one to another. None saw anything unusual. The stranger then took the acorn and inserted it carefully into a small crack in the floorboards. Immediately there was a great sound of cracking and splintering and an oak sapling burst out of the floor and rose quickly upwards. In no time at all its trunk grew thick and round and its branches burst into leaf and spread so that Sir Robert and his guests were unable to even see the ceiling of the hall. Buds burst from the branches and then many acorns quickly swelled and dropped down upon the heads of the assembly, to their amazement.

Sir Robert was greatly amused and clapped his hands. He instructed his servants to bring his prize hog into the hall. When it was brought in everyone saw that it was a huge and magnificent beast, almost the size of a heifer. On entering the hall it immediately fell to and feasted on the piles of young acorns, eating them all up.

Now, said Sir Robert, how will we eat our dinner? For the tree filled the hall and there was no room for the tables.

The stranger shrugged and replied, it must be cut down.

And so, Sir Robert ordered his men bring axes and cut the tree down, which they did. And with great effort it was dragged outside into the garden and the floor swept clean. Then the tables were set and the feast began.

To celebrate his new title Sir Robert had planned an elaborate banquet with many courses. Dish after dish were brought to the tables and he emptied his cellars of his very best wines. As they ate the guests saw that the prize hog had been slaughtered and was set on the spit roast in the huge fireplace that dominated one end of the hall. It was so big that it took three men to turn the spit. After many courses of fish and various small birds, the hog was carved and on eating it each of the guests remarked that its flavour was remarkable.

Now, at the end of the meal, the stranger stood up once more and everyone fell silent.

My Lord, he said, I would like to propose a toast.

The servants hurriedly filled the glasses of the guests and they all stood to honour their host. However, the stranger clapped his hands and immediately all the guests felt that they were rooted to the spot where they stood. Indeed, their legs and feet were transformed into the roots of young oak trees and quickly found their way through the cracks between the floorboards and into the soil below, and their arms became branches, bearing leaves and buds and spreading wide. The *servants looked on in astonishment. Sir Robert, who was sat at the head of the table on a great chair that resembled a throne, was also stricken. Oak leaves began to sprout from beneath his fingernails, and green tendrils emerged from his mouth and nose and even from his eyes, wrapping themselves about the arms of the chair and so securing him in place, even though he struggled and cried out. A profusion of foliage appeared all about him until after just a few moments it was no longer possible to tell where man ended and tree began. Indeed, the hall quickly came to resemble a dark and tangled wood and some of the branches even burst up through the ceiling to reveal the night sky, full of stars. Confronted with this spectacle, the servants all fled and some, as they left the hall, noted that all trace of the great oak tree had disappeared, along with any sign of the stranger.*

No one knew who that man was, and he was never seen again. Some speculated that he had been hired by one of those wronged by Sir Robert, to enact a deserved revenge, for Sir Robert had done terrible things in his time.

After this, Sir Robert's estate quickly fell into a state of ruinous disrepair. The fields and gardens were untended and the hall soon began to crumble. No one went there, for it had a reputation as a spell-stricken place. But some curious visitors who were brave enough to approach would go to look on the spectacle of the hall, its roof open to the sky and a dense throng of oak trees filling its every space, pushing out through the windows and doorways. With time this became a celebrated spectacle and in 1636 Hans Richardson made an engraving of it, which proved very popular.

From John Evelyn, *Sylva, or A Discourse on Forest Trees*
(the edition of 1776)

*

147

Birth. The most disturbing transformation in Ovid's *Metamorphoses* is that of Myrrha. The change is doubly disquieting for the cause, incest, and the precise condition of Myrrha, who is nine months pregnant when it occurs.

Myrrha is a beautiful young woman. Her tragedy is that she falls passionately in love with her own father, King Cinyras. Ovid allows Myrrha a long monologue in which she agonises over her predicament and it is clear that she is fully aware of the grotesque implications of her emotions. Then, with the horrified assistance of her nurse, the king is tricked and incest is committed. In darkness, to hide the crime, again and again it happens, night after night, until finally Cinyras resolves that he will see the face of his young lover. Entering the bed chamber with a torch he discovers what has passed and takes up a sword in fury to kill his daughter (and himself too, perhaps?). However, Myrrha flees and, so we are told, wanders the lands for nine months, finally arriving in a place called Saba.

In shame and self-loathing, she prays to the gods, saying that she deserves to be punished; she should not be allowed to live, for if she does her existence will debase all living things. However, she pleads, neither should she be allowed to bring shame upon the dead. The gods, she says, should refuse her life and refuse her death by changing her form. Ovid says, 'some god did listen.'

The transformation is vivid. The earth closes over her feet and roots stretch forth from her nails, her bones become hard (though, in a peculiar detail, Ovid says the marrow remained) and her blood turns to sap. Her arms are changed into long branches and her fingers to twigs. Her soft skin hardens to bark about her heavy womb.

I think of the details in the description: the cracking toenails, the stiffening muscles, the slowing blood becoming golden sap, and the beautiful young woman bowing her head to welcome the change sweeping over her.

There then follows something even more extraordinary. Ovid tells us that Myrrha's baby was now ready to be born. Cracks appeared in the bark and the tree was split open – picture the ripping and tearing and splintering of the tree trunk – to reveal the fresh wood within, the arboreal musculature, that strange pale pink-yellow of new growth, and a baby boy, flecked with sticky sap, golden in the sunlight, fragrant. No blood. Sap. Adonis.

Dust. Gramper used to say, we are all dust. But it is only now, so many years later, that I think I understand what he meant.

We had several dictionaries, and in one of them I found this peculiar example of usage: 'The dictionaries were covered in *dust.*'

Elsewhere, within those disintegrating pages: *something worthless, very small particles of earth or sand. A fine powder which consists of very small particles of a substance such as gold, wood or coal. A fine dry powder consisting of earth or waste matter lying on the ground or on surfaces or carried in the air. Fine particles of matter (as of earth). Spilth. The particles into which something disintegrates. Dirt, sand, flakes or filth. Soot, ashes. Dried earth reduced to powder. A cloud of finely powdered earth or other matter in the air. The surface of the ground. A fine dry powder. Chaff.*

And this too: *the earth, as the resting place of the dead. The earthly remains of bodies once alive; the remains of the human body.*

149

Debris. The shadow of life.

Dust, borne on the air currents: ancient pollen, fugitive minerals, pre-solar grains, silts ground from the floor tiles by centuries of incessant footfall, even irons and silicates (the only trace remains of burning meteorites immolated at the end of unimaginable journeys). In paper fibres too, as if the pages of the book itself, the one you are holding even now, are succumbing to entropy (which of course, like all things, they are) and shrouding themselves. Structure must dissipate.

The dust says, all that is solid will break down.

How much time do you need?

As I write, dead cells settle upon me and upon everything I can see, particles of skin and hair from the people who have lived in this house before me, and their ancestors too. Carbon that once formed the eye of a bird or the leaves of the ferns that thrived deep in a primeval forest. Hundreds of thousands of years. Millions of years. Spinning. Spiralling. Drifting. Adrift. Motes containing traces of hydrogen and lithium from the beginning of everything tumble in the unstill air.

The unravelling universe forms a spectral veil which flows slowly through these rooms. If the daylight comes in at the correct angle I can see a spiral galaxy, a supernova, a shooting star burning to pieces as it enters our atmosphere; a halo.

What Gramper meant, I now think, is not only that we, like all living things, will one day be dust. But that we also come *from* dust. All matter is in the grip of transformation. We *are* dust. It is dust that courses through our veins.

I find the notion comforting.

*

Alchemy. We gathered apples in the ruined orchard, our breath clouding the cool air, and carried them home in an old basket. 'And now,' said Mother, with uncharacteristic flair, wearing a cunning smile and with a definite sparkle in her eyes, 'you are about to witness an alchemical miracle, the transformation, nay the *transmutation*, of base materials – flour, butter, fruit – into a completely new and divine assembly.'

She read the confusion upon my face.

'Apple pie!' she exclaimed. 'Apple pie! From the apples that have grown all year long, nourished by the sun and the rain, we're going to bake a delicious pie for our supper. We're going to take these humble ingredients' – she paused to take a bag of flour from the larder and to pull the butter dish from the fridge – 'and transform them through the mysteries of the culinary arts into something beautiful and delicious. I am going to show you how to do it.' She leant in and kissed my forehead.

I am sitting at the kitchen table and my feet don't quite reach the floor. In my mind's eye it is autumn. The leaves on the trees beyond the window are burnished, russet and ochre, flecks of burgundy. A low sun and long shadows across the flags of the kitchen floor. She stands between the table and the sink, with light coming through the window behind her so that she seems to have a fiery aura about her. It is a Sunday, I think. A day of rest and reflection. The cat is asleep in its basket beside the woodburner. The house is quiet. We have been walking up on the heath and on our way back we visited the old orchard and gathered the apples.

'First we must peel,' she said. The apples were firm but brown and many were scabbed or marked from where they had lain in the damp grass. She deftly peeled, cored and chopped them into a large bowl, humming a vague tune as she did so. A sprinkle of cider vinegar – to keep them from going brown as they wait for us, she explained – and I was instructed to turn them over with a wooden spoon, to make sure they were well coated.

Next, she measured flour and butter into a mixing bowl, added sugar and a pinch of salt, and churned it all together. It quickly coagulated into a gooey mass. A little more flour. When it was solid but still pliable, she dusted the tabletop with flour and turned it out. I was allowed to knead the pastry and to then roll it out into a sheet using a heavy rolling pin.

The apple chunks went into the pie dish, were dusted with cinnamon and sugar, and the sheet of pastry was draped over and trimmed with a knife. She used a fork to seal the edges. She then rolled the spare pastry out again and instructed me to cut decorations for the pie from it. I carefully carved a series of leaves, incising the stems and veins, and then from the last remnants cut a stylised loveheart.

She used egg yolk to fix the decorations in place.

'This is very appropriate. In ancient Greece the gift of an apple was a popular way to declare one's devotion. It was one of the attributes of Aphrodite, the goddess of love. Old Theokritos of Syrakousa said that apples were first discovered by Dionysius. That old rogue, the god of wine and madness, had many names and one of them means *he-in-the-tree.*'

She washed the top of the pastry with yolk and prepared to put the pie in the oven. 'What else do we know about apples?'

'The Tree of Knowledge?' I suggested. I was thinking also of the blood red apple, the poisoned apple, that the evil queen offers to Snow White.

'Yes, that's the most famous apple tree of all. But did you know,' she said, 'that there is no mention of an apple in the story of Adam and Eve? Scholars have suggested that the Tree of Knowledge was perhaps a fig tree or even a pomegranate.'

Of course, I didn't know anything about that. It was an apple that Eve had eaten, thereby causing the Fall and all the trouble, the pain and tears, that had persisted ever since.

The pie went into the oven and soon the house was filled with sweet perfume. Mother washed up and outside the light began to fade.

When the pie came out, the crust was golden and my pastry leaves were a beautiful autumn brown, curling at the edges. Apple juice had bubbled out from beneath the pastry and steam jetted from the little holes Mother had made with a fork. The aroma was divine, transporting, overwhelming.

We ate the fruit of the Tree of Knowledge, hot and sweet and tangy, and gave thanks to Old Green Jack – *he-in-the-tree*, we joked – who Mother claimed was the spirit that looked after the trees in the ruined orchard.

Dear Friend,

I was so excited to read of your success. I always knew you would do something wonderful. I ordered a copy of your book about the marshes and it sits prominently on my coffee table, like a trophy. Whenever my friends visit I push it into their hands and insist they look through it. Your paintings are so delicate and patient. It is extraordinary.

You wrote that you are preparing for an exhibition. Where will it be?

You ask what I remember of the great storm. Well, it wasn't so bad for us as we were inland, but it was still pretty impressive. We knew it was coming; I seem to remember a big build-up to it. Every day for a week the weather just got worse and worse and there were warnings on the radio. Dad was really worried. He was even convinced there would be heavy snow. When it finally arrived and he realised just how strong the winds were he was scared that the chicken runs would be blown open and so we had to carry the birds in and put them into makeshift pens in the barn for the night. The wind was amazing. As we carried them in we had to lean into the gale so as not to be bowled over. The birds were strangely subdued. You could just pick them up off the ground and carry them under your arms. Then, because we'd brought in the chickens, Mum said we should bring in the sheep too. That was trickier but we got them in from the fields and put them in with the goats. It was all rather exciting, to be honest.

I remember that night sitting up and looking out of my bedroom window across the fields. The whole landscape appeared to be in motion, whipped by the wind and scoured by swirling blasts of rain. The lights from the house lit it up to the edge of the garden but every minute or so lightning illuminated the whole land with sharp light and I could see for miles and miles and it looked like it was just black and white. The crackles of thunder came, always closer and louder than expected.

It was certainly the strongest and wildest storm I've ever seen.

The next day it was amazing to see how many trees had come down. The roads to our village were blocked and we were cut off. That was exciting too, in a way – like the times we were snowed in. There was such a mess. Flooding everywhere. It was like a giant had come and trampled through the garden. Everything was broken. Dad insisted that I stay and help to clear up with Mum. I was dying to get down to the coast to see you, but I couldn't. Of course, the phone lines were down. I think even the radio was out.

So it was a couple of days before I saw you and it was all over by then and we were getting back to normal. But I do remember that you were a little distracted, even by your own high standards.

Around that time there was the whale. Do you remember? We went to see it, didn't we? I have a memory of us smoking cigarettes in the shelter of the dunes while they cut it open.

What about Jack? Did you know that I kissed him once? He sometimes seemed so much older than us, but he wasn't really. Just a couple of years. Older but not wiser, I would say. Back then you and I thought we knew more than everyone else put together. I wonder what happened to Jack. I guess he is still there. Probably with a wife and kids, still doing his thing, whatever that is. Fishing or farming. I knew we would be the only ones to escape. The gravity of that place is so strong. I imagine they're all still there. Older, smaller, wondering what might have been.

Do you ever go back? I don't know if I could. Not now. It's funny though, looking through your book, it brings that place back in a way I haven't felt before. I'm amazed by how many of the names of flowers and herbs I still know.

I have some news for you which I know will make you smile. I am to play Miranda. Can you imagine?

In your book I discovered a marsh plant called Prospero's Promise and I should like to find one and wear a sprig in my hair when I am on stage.

Write more. Don't disappear again.

With love,

Quill

*

Wood that longs to be human. Carlo Collodi's story of *Pinocchio* (the original tale first published in book form in 1883, not the wondrous Disney animation of 1940) contains a number of elements from my story, most notably a transformation or transformations, as well as a whale and an absent father. The central metamorphosis is unusual in that it goes in the opposite direction to those in Ovid: a piece of wood, 'not a grand piece of wood, it was only a common log', is imbued with sentience and longs to become a human boy. Geppetto, the toymaker, makes the wood into a puppet and names him Pinocchio. Pinocchio has many adventures before he finally realises his ambition.

At one point in the story he sprouts donkey ears, becomes an ass and is sold to the ringmaster of a circus. Pinocchio's life as a donkey is horrific. He is constantly whipped and starved. Eventually he lames himself during a performance and is sold for twenty pence to a man who intends to use his skin to make a drum. This man ties a stone to Pinocchio's leg and pushes him into the sea, hoping to drown him. After leaving him for fifty minutes beneath the water he pulls him out and is astonished to find he has changed back into a puppet.

The man cries out, 'But how can you, who but a short time ago, were a little donkey, have become a wooden puppet, only from having been left in the water?'

Pinocchio replies: 'It must have been the effect of the sea-water. The sea makes extraordinary changes.'

He is then swallowed by a sea monster, a huge whale, and deep in its belly he finds again Geppetto, his lost 'father', and helps him escape. Geppetto is the wooden child's father only inasmuch as he is its carver, and has been absent for most of the tale. However, it should be noted that this absence is not of his own volition. He has been left behind by the mischievous, credulous and wandering Pinocchio. The rescue, this good deed, is perhaps the redemptive moment and the catalyst for an understanding of morality that allows Pinocchio's final transformation.

It is a fairy tale and therefore contains no such thing as irony. Everything is a metaphor and is presented at face value. The most extraordinary events are not questioned. The transformations are just stages in the development from larva to pupa to butterfly. The rewards of one's actions are reaped. It is, in short, an absurdist moral fable.

There is also a very odd Czech folk tale which has echoes of *Pinocchio*. As in Collodi's strange story, a piece of wood acquires unruly life. It is sometimes called 'The Long-Desired Child' or, more simply, 'Otesánek'. Karel Jaromír Erben first wrote it down in the late nineteenth century.

In a village deep in the forest a couple lived in a small cottage. They were very poor. The man was a labourer and the woman spun cloth. They were childless and wished for nothing more than to have a child they could call their own. However, their neighbours said to them, 'Thank the heavens you do not have a child, for you do not even have enough food to feed yourselves.' That was how poor they were.

One day, the man was digging out tree stumps in the forest and he came across a mandrake-like root which looked strangely like a little child; it had a head, body, arms and legs. Knots and gnarls in the bark made eyes and mouth. And so, he took his axe and cut it free. Thinking it would comfort her, he took the root home and made a gift of it to his wife, and they called it Otesánek. She was delighted and wrapped it in cloth and sang to it.

Suddenly, Otesánek began to kick and scream, crying 'Mother, I want something to eat!'

The woman was beside herself with joy and prepared food for her baby. It ate it all up and screamed for more. She went to a neighbour and bought milk and Otesánek drank it all up and screamed for more. Next she went to the village and borrowed a loaf of bread and when she got home she put it on the table and went to get things to make soup with. Seeing it, Otesánek scrambled out of the swaddling cloths, jumped on the table, ate up the bread and then screamed for more. 'Have mercy upon us,' cried the woman when she returned. 'Have you eaten all the bread?'

'Yes, Mother,' replied the wooden child. 'I have eaten it, and now I will eat you too.' He opened his mouth and swallowed her up. When the man returned home from his work in the forest, he ate him up too. Then, seeing that there was nothing more to eat in the little hut, he went into the village to see what he might find. There he ate up a young girl pushing a wheelbarrow, a peasant and the horses and cart he was driving, and then a shepherd, his sheepdog and the flock of sheep he was tending. With everything he ate, Otesánek got bigger and bigger.

Finally, he came to an old woman in a field tending to her cabbages. Without pausing, he pulled them all from the ground and ate them.

The old woman was angry and cried out, 'Otesánek, you monster! Surely you have eaten enough now to be satisfied?'

Otesánek looked at her and a horrible grin appeared on his woody face. 'No,' he said. 'I am an eater and I will eat you too!'

But the old woman was too quick for him. As he eyed her up and tried to decide if he would eat her legs or arms first, she took her hoe, which was very sharp, and struck him a blow that split him in half. Otesánek immediately fell down dead, and was just a stump of wood again. But out of his cloven body sprang all the people and things – the sheep, the sheepdog, the shepherd, the horse and cart and so on, and eventually even his mother and father too. After that, they never once again lamented that they did not have a child.

Roots. In an old herbarium I read up about mandrakes, and then later endured a strange dream. I am having a lot of them lately.

The roots of the mandrake or *Mandragora* were once highly prized for their narcotic, hypnotic, aphrodisiacal and hallucinogenic powers and changed hands for huge sums of money. But they were also feared. As the roots often form a semblance of a human figure – as do the bifurcated tubers of commonplace carrots and parsnips growing in stony soils – many superstitions grew up around them. In the Middle Ages, it was widely believed that if you pulled up a mandrake it would emit a horrific scream and you would be instantly killed. For this reason, there were various elaborate strategies for the harvesting of mandrakes. One was to take a black dog and tie his tail to the root with a length of rope. Having carefully blocked your ears with wax you would take a tasty morsel and toss it before the hound, which would lunge for it and in doing so pull the rooted man-plant from the ground and seal its own fate. Once out of the earth the mandrake was supposedly harmless and could be handled freely, and might prove an extremely profitable prize. It could be ground up and sold as an aphrodisiac or carved into an amulet that would bring the bearer good luck.

The illustrations of mandrakes from medieval herbals and magical tomes are rather charming. The mandrake is invariably depicted as a tiny person buried in the earth, usually with only head and shoulders visible. A profusion of leaves and flowers issues forth from the creature's head, like an unruly outgrowth of hair. But sometimes scale shifts and the mandrake stands still upon the earth, his feet rooted, branches and leaves shooting up from his head and shoulders.

In my dream I am buried in the soil. I feel it pressed against my skin. I feel it. Granular. Cold. I feel the dampness of the earth. I cannot move. I begin to 'sprout'. It is not unpleasant.

Ice. A huge iceberg like a polished blue crystal palace has travelled from far away and arrived at the North Shore and, like a sentient being, has made its slow way into the creek that cuts across the marshes to the little harbour quay. People come from miles around to see the extraordinary spectacle. It radiates coldness, as a fire gives off heat. I can feel it on my face: a gentle prickling. It is an augur from the Arctic. In the dream I can see my face reflected in the glassy surface of the ice, as it rocks gently in the brown water, but the face is unfamiliar and I am not sure if it is a boy or a girl that looks back at me.

I stand on the edge of the quay, the water flowing past me, and the great iceberg glimmers and glistens, an impossible mass. I fancy I see tendrils of frost coating the weeds that sprout in the brick wall of the quay, and then spreading across the marsh, riming the reeds and stilling the waters.

I often dream of icebergs, immaculate and implacable. If it is not wood – leaves, branches and unruly roots – it is ice, pure and white.

The Great Frost of 1709, which spread throughout Western Europe, began in early January and lasted three months, with profound effects felt for the whole of the following year. It was reportedly the coldest period in Europe in half a millennium. In France, the Atlantic coast and River Seine froze, crops failed, and many thousands of Parisians died. Closer to home, the rivers of East Anglia were stopped. Floating ice entered the North Sea and menaced shipping for the first time in memory.

That same year, when the ice was biting hardest, some way further down the coast across the county border at Aldeburgh, the wonderfully named composer William Babell, working on his *3rd Book of the Ladys Entertainment, or Banquet of Musick*, a collection of pleasant harpsichord arrangements, reported to friends that he had had to give up his work as the ink in his well had frozen solid.

Somewhere else. Dull days. Boring days. Days when nothing ever happened: just the sea coming and going, the wind blowing, and the sun's slow journey across the sky. The waxing and waning of the moon. Time stretching out like an infinite piece of elastic. Hours that are like days. Days that extend into weeks. Weeks that feel like months. The winter term that never ends. The endless summer holidays. The nagging sensation that one is out of time, in a place beyond time. The sense that life – real life, modern life, whatever that is – was ongoing somewhere else, in the distant towns and cities, and that there, on the edge of the sea, things have been caught, stilled.

Do the hands of the clock turn more slowly at the edge of things than they do at the centre? It seemed to me then that they did. Sometimes it seemed that they did not turn at all.

Echoes. Why do I hoard these stories, and the artworks that show them? Perhaps it is because they are all more or less versions – or variations – of this story. My story. Or is it that the tale is a kind of commentary on the artworks and stories? They are echoes of each other, perhaps. Or not exactly echoes, for an echo comes after the fact, but more like premonitions. Stories from the past that reflect upon the present.

In gathering together all this material, what did I learn? What did I discover? That, as Heraclitus tells us, we may not step into the same river twice. That all things, be they objects, people or places, are in flux and that this is an unending process. That one cannot resist this unending process but must go along with it, even embrace it. For why might not a stone become a bird, a leaf become a bee, a tree become a man, or vice versa?

The Tempest. The play ends with an extraordinary reveal, in which the veils that mark the boundaries between fiction and reality are successively stripped away. Ariel is set free.

Deceptions and transformations have abounded throughout the play, and of course the play is an illusion too, a kind of embodied hallucination. Prospero says as much in the final act, when in a very beautiful and famous speech, he reveals that we have been witnesses to a fictive and dramatic construction, an illusion now 'melted into air, into thin air'.

But that is not all, for in the epilogue that follows the finale of the drama and which is the conclusion of the play, Prospero reappears and explains that his magical powers have now vanished – the implication is that he is now a mere actor standing before us rather than the great magician – and he must ask the audience to send him home with their applause:

> . . . *release me from my bands*
> *With the help of your good hands.*

The final line of the play is Prospero's entreaty to us: 'Let your indulgence set me free'. He is speaking now not only as Prospero but moreover, perhaps, also as the playwright himself who has crafted the speech and the entire dramatic construction that went before. At that moment multiple fictions collapse into a singular reality.

Many have speculated that this speech is Shakespeare himself, at the end of his final play, announcing his retirement from the theatre.

After many years of experience I know now that such vanishings and illusions, such dramatic mirages and misunderstandings, can perhaps even happen in real life, beyond the stage and the walls of the theatre. Nothing is as it first seems.

Everything shifts and flows.
So it goes.

V

ARIEL

Full fathom five thy father lies,
Of his bones are coral made;
Those are pearls that were his eyes;
Nothing of him that doth fade,
But doth suffer a sea-change
Into something rich and strange.

'Ariel's Song', *The Tempest*

I let things drift for a few years, turning it all over in my mind and collecting the stories and artworks that cast a light on what had – or what might have – happened. I knew I would have to go back. I had to see if the images in my mind's eye were phantoms or if they were real. As time passed I became more and more doubtful as to the authenticity of my memories; everything was beginning to feel unstable and I no longer knew which version of the story to have faith in. Yet it did seem imperative that I believe in one of them. I could not carry on in such a state of infinite doubt. So, one fine spring day, I closed up my studio and boarded a train back to the North Shore.

It was many years since I had been beneath those big skies. Mother had died long before and afterwards I had turned my back on that old country and made a life elsewhere. When she went, I let the ties that bound me to that place and to my young life there, and even to Quill, loosen and fall away. The passing of a parent is a profound experience and in some ways it offers a chance to begin again. While our parents are with us we are always their children, no matter our age. But when they are gone we have the chance to be the person that we really are, free of constraining influence. I had always felt a need to appear and behave in a certain way so as not to worry my dear mother, who was so careful and nervous about so many things. With her passing something shifted. I had made a life in a big city and had become, perhaps, a new version of myself. I had a career, a living, a home and, as a consequence, an (admittedly fragile) sense of equilibrium. However, while the past had retreated and the marshes and the sea coast seemed ever more distant, they were always present, like a shadow. My own shadow, perhaps; sometimes behind and sometimes before, depending on the position of the sun, a second version of me, thin and insubstantial. When people asked me where I came from, I would hesitate to answer; it didn't seem quite right to name the city in which I then lived. I knew that if you were to cut me open I would bleed salt water, marsh seep, clay creep and black mud. Inside me you would find shingle, silt and seashells, lumps of driftwood instead of bones, seaweed, tangles of old rope and knots of twine for guts and nerves, nodules of flint, pine cones and acorns, and sprays of forget-me-nots as blue as the sky, grasses, reeds, loosestrife and knapweed. For I am of that place, and always will be.

I planned my journey carefully. I left in the morning, with only a small rucksack containing a change of clothes, a rain jacket, notebooks and pencils and a folder containing Mother's translations of Ovid, which I was once again working on illustrations for. At about midday, the train pulled into the old city. With time to spare before the next stage of the journey out to the coast, I left the station, crossed the slow dark Wensum and followed the riverbank to Pull's Ferry, a medieval flint tower and water gate. The water of the river was clear and fronds of weed swayed and waved lazily. The sun was shining and the scent of blossom was in the air, carried from somewhere nearby by a soft breeze. Brilliant yellow daffodils – Narcissus's flower – crowded the banks and the river. It was beautiful, like one of those enchanted days of childhood. I had the curious sensation of moving backwards in time. For a brief moment I thought the water was perhaps flowing in the wrong direction.

From the river I wandered through quiet streets up into the cathedral quarter, with the great spire towering above. Although I had not been in the city for many years, I knew the way. Everything was familiar. In the cloisters I found what I had come to see: the Green Men.

That great cathedral contains over a thousand intricately carved and coloured stone roof bosses. Many hang high up in the vast nave and the side chapels but in the cloisters where the roof is lower one can see all the wonderful detail of them. Bible stories predominate but among them are a number of extraordinary faces, pagan insurgents bursting into unruly foliage. Some sprout leaves and tendrils straight from the flesh of forehead, cheek and chin, from others it rushes forth from wide open mouths. They have looked down at the business of the cloister – and the crowds of curious tourists – for over eight hundred years with an attitude of peculiar attentiveness and floral vitality. They seem alive, truly remarkable examples of the stonemason's art: the inanimate rendered animate, transformed. I remembered visiting the cathedral as a small child and being fascinated by these peculiar foliate beings, contemplating me with neither displeasure nor approval, so surely not of church but not of the real world neither. I was happy to see them again after so many years.

After making several slow circuits of the cloister square, I stopped and examined one extraordinary head in detail. He must have been recently restored as the paintwork was bright and there were veins of gold leaf that ran through the leaves that crowned his grinning face. Foliage formed out of his eyebrows and forehead but was also bursting out of his wide mouth. He did not appear to be in pain; it looked instead like a kind of ecstasy. He was grinning or perhaps singing, fierce and alert. Was it like taking a drug, I wondered, feeling the change invade your body through vein and nerve, spreading from a central point, a glimmering focus?

Might it even be possible, I wondered, by sheer willpower, to induce such a transformation in oneself? Might there be spells, now long forgotten: a form of *rough magic* that might do the trick?

As I moved on, I wondered, where are the Green Women?

I looked again and, yes, they were all men. Some were curiously androgynous and others were too obscured by their leafy mutations for me to be sure, but it seemed that they were all male.

After walking the circuit a few more times, I returned to the station and climbed onto the small two-carriage train that would carry me east on the branch line that runs out to the coast. The train was slow, winding out through the watery regions, past rivers, lakes and woods, before making towards the rolling land that fringes the coast, stopping at many little towns and villages with vaguely familiar names. As such, my journey of just thirty miles or so took an eternity. Once again I had that remarkable sensation of travelling back in time, of unspooling towards a distant singularity.

On the train I entered a reverie. I sat perfectly still, though jostled by the bumping and rattling motion, my face close against the cool glass. At first a million thoughts and worries were in my head, but slowly they evaporated. The countryside was lit with bright sunshine, but off in the distance, towards the coast and further north, the sky was a peculiar dark blue. A drop of Prussian blue ink had suffused a sheet of wet blotting paper, and now the sublime darkness spread through the fabric of the sheet before finally fading. Water and air and wind. Something abstract was hanging in the sky like an augur.

At every station I watched the other travellers keenly, seized by an irrational fear that someone from the past would climb on and recognise me, maybe even challenge me. What right did I have to come back?

Wild roses swayed as the train bundled past. Young wheat in the fields, rippled by the wind. Did I imagine it, that the light became brighter as we neared the sea?

Eventually the train arrived at the end of the line, at a once-popular but faded resort town. As I did not want to rush the journey, I did not push on. I needed to acclimatise. Like a diver returning from a sojourn deep beneath the ocean, who must pause to balance the gases in the bloodstream or risk a calamitous attack of the bends, I needed to take my time.

I had telephoned and booked a room at an inn on the seafront. I had fond memories of drinking pints and laughing in the bar there when I was a teenager – a vivid memory of flushed faces, cider, cigarettes and a jukebox that had only two or three good songs that were played over and over again – but when I arrived the place was completely unfamiliar; it didn't correspond to that memory-summoned venue and I became convinced that this was not the same place at all. I wondered if it had actually existed or if it was perhaps another fiction conjured somewhere in those intervening years.

I had a drink in the bar, then bought fish and chips on the high street and carried them down to the seafront where

I ate them on a bench overlooking the gaudy pier. Dusk was coming, and the sea was a stony grey. Nothing moved out there, as far as I could see, although I knew that somewhere in the pale expanse the rigs crouched like bristling insects. Monstrous seagulls watched me balefully from a railing, waiting.

Contemplating the sea, I remembered a sailing expedition taken with Father. I was still very young, at primary school, and at that time he had a small skiff. It was to be my first trip out and I was very excited. I remember Mother made up a picnic hamper and I was thrilled by the prospect of eating lunch not on land but somewhere out on the water. In my mind, Father and I were to be explorers, crossing a great ocean for the very first time. I was thinking too of the men who were even then sailing out into the void of space aboard the early space capsules, the Geminis and the Mercuries, protected from the nothingness only by a thin skin of metal, little more than a tin can. As I imagined our impending voyage, I felt a connection. I would be one of them.

The boat was moored in the quay and I sat in the prow while Father set everything up. Mother watched, smiling, from the harbour wall. Then we were off, and she was waving to us, quickly becoming smaller, and I was waving back. I remembered being surprised by the speed with which we raced along the dike and out through the marshes. Caught on the air currents. Suddenly we were beyond and heading into the void and everything changed. The water, which had been calm and smooth in the channel, became rough and the little boat bucked and shuddered. Father laughed with joy and I thought that I had never seen him look so happy.

I looked back and saw the land receding. I could see the village and the church tower on the hill, but it was all quickly reduced to a narrow line along the horizon, a surprisingly tenuous border between the sea and the sky. It was shrinking, leaving only the air above and the thin surface of the water below, across which we raced. As we sped out into that expanse of space I felt a growing sense of fear, which I tried very hard not to let Father see. But I needn't have worried; he was busy giving me a running commentary on our progress and happily explaining the names and purposes of all the different parts of the boat.

Eventually, Father deemed us to be far enough out and took the sail in, so that we slowed and then drifted. There was nothing out there. Nothing. Just the grey water and the pale sky above.

'Isn't it beautiful!' he exclaimed.

I nodded and tried to smile, but tears were coming.

Father came and sat next to me, causing the boat to shift alarmingly, and opened up the hamper.

I thought of all the emptiness around us. I thought of the great deeps that were below us, a vast darkness teeming with unknown and unseen beasts. Who could know what might be lurking there, just below our fragile vessel, hanging in the shadows, waiting, biding its time? The sense of vertical space, above and below us, combined with the lack of any other thing visible on the horizontal plain, and the perceived fragility of our little boat became utterly terrifying to me.

Father was unwrapping our sandwiches when he saw me. I was crying, silently. He looked at me, surprised.

'What is it?' he asked.

173

'I'm scared,' I whispered. 'Can we go back now?'

He frowned. 'But it's beautiful,' he said. 'Isn't it?'

I shook my head, conscious that I had failed an important test.

He was furious. He took the sandwiches Mother had carefully prepared for us and hurled them from the boat.

We tacked back in silence, and it took an age.

Things go round and round. I think now of Father and how he left, and the curious vacancy in my life, the hollow at the heart of our small family. Yet he had experienced something similar. He too was an only child and he too had been abandoned by his own father. I can't say I really knew the story, but I did know that when he referred to my grandfather, it was with anger and bitterness in his voice. Father felt wronged. Despite that, he was compelled to repeat the mistake (although of course I cannot truly call it a mistake and I don't know even now if, afterwards, he thought that he had done the right or the wrong thing in leaving us).

In the morning I was one of just three to board the first steam train of the day to travel the eight-mile stretch along the coast and then inland over the heath to the town. The steam train runs on a ghost line restored by enthusiasts and operated mainly for summer tourists. The sense of moving backwards into another era was acute. When a conductor in Victorian uniform stepped into the carriage to check my ticket, I felt a weird but absolute *dyschronia*.

At the end of the line I disembarked, feeling that I was stepping into another world.

The market town was the same as it had always been. I

followed a well-remembered road to the edge of the houses and stepped through an opening in a hedge onto an old track leading through oak woods. From there I emerged onto the heath, where the gorse flowers were bright yellow in the sun, and then went down the steep hill to the coast track. That place was coming back to me; the marshes looked magnificent in their austere beauty. The sea shimmered beyond. There were many birds crowding the edge of the ponds and scrapes. It was magnificent, desolate. The now-unfamiliar horizontality was unnerving. The arching sky was infinite. It was empty and bleak, but the landscape held the unusual and affecting beauty it always had.

From the coast track I looked for and then followed a path through the reeds and eventually came out at the shingle. I climbed the bank and the sea was there before me. The same as it ever was. It was the sea of my childhood and yet it was not. This was not the same water; it could not be. The churning of the sea and the sucking and pulling of the tides meant that the water I watched as a child might now be washing against a cliff in South America, or roiling in an unfathomably deep trench in the midst of the Pacific. A peculiar notion; this flow of all things.

I turned north and followed the shingle and sand, with the waves gently lapping and swashing at my right ear, and in this way I came eventually to the place where the whale had beached. There was no trace of that terrible event. The sand was smooth and even and the hollow in which it had lain, which had filled with seawater and blood, was long gone. But at the top of the beach, where the grasses were, there was a cairn, like a votive sculpture. Pieces of driftwood had been bound together with orange and blue twine and driven into the sand. Stones and shells were piled up against the structure, giving it stability. Seaweed had been draped over it and feathers and reeds had been inserted into the gaps between the wood, giving the whole thing a bristling appearance, like an enlarged seed head. I sat beside it and remembered the whale. Quill had said she was there that day, but she had not been, at least not in my version of things.

I scanned the beach for the right stone. I found a nodule of flint like a hen's egg, which nestled comfortably inside my hand, and carefully placed it on the top of the cairn. It was a kind of offering. I walked on.

Finally, I came to the place where I had found him. The shingle banks undulated and there were curving trails of debris along the high tide lines: seaweed, driftwood, broken crab shells. As the village came into view I stopped and then realised I was standing in the place. There appeared to be a kind of shadow upon the shingle there, like a stain, but it was perhaps just a trick of the light. There was a broad and shallow depression, a kind of bowl, in which flotsam had been held: an old boot, coils of rubbery seaweed, the remains of a broken lobster trap, the rotting wing of a grey gull. I paused. Could one make a man from such things? The sea was the same, washing backwards and forwards. I looked out and wondered again, as I had done countless times before, where he had come from and by what design he had arrived here, in this precise place, and if it was possible that I had in some way summoned him up from the sea.

In Ralph of Coggeshall's account of the 'wild man' who had been taken from the sea at Orford, there was a peculiar phrase which I kept coming back to. Ralph had conjectured that the creature might have been 'an evil spirit hiding in the body of some drowned man'. He said that such a phenomenon had been previously reported in an account of the life of Saint Owen (something that I had tried but failed to find). A dead body, drifting in the salt water, animated by a vagrant spirit; it was an extraordinary idea, and one that had haunted many of my dreams.

Carrying on into a landscape that itself was like something from a dream, I cut inland on the marsh path. My fingertips were tingling and I began to realise how much I had invested in this moment. I was nervous with anticipation but also with a kind of dread. But the sun was shining and the village was there, with the church tower still pointing straight up to heaven, as it had done for so many hundreds of years.

As I approached, I wondered about Jack. Was he still here, greying hair and slack body, working one of the farms or helping on one of the last boats that still went out? I wondered if I would recognise him if we were to meet. What might we say to one another? It was funny to think of. So much time had passed.

Alice Fitch, I supposed, would long since have passed on. But what about Bill and Marge and the others? I saw them all, lined up, as if posed for a school photograph. In her letter, Quill had proclaimed that only we two had escaped, but how would she know if she had not been back?

At the Green I saw that the pub was not called The Green Man and wondered if I had indulged in poetic licence when writing of it. It was called The Black Dog which, all things considered, is a good name for this stretch of the coast: a conjuring of the shadow. It was a fine day and some people were sitting on benches outside, drinking and talking. They were walkers and birders, booted, jacketed and festooned with binoculars and camera gear. The pub sign showed a huge black dog, silhouetted, looking out across the marshes, a dead hare at his feet.

The pub had been renovated. It was now smart and modern, full of pine and exposed brickwork. Blackboards listed the menu and the beers available. A log fire burned in the grate. As I suspected, it bore no resemblance to the image I had been holding firmly and affectionately in my mind. I took a seat at the bar and a young woman with a nose piercing asked me what I would like. I ordered wine and asked for a menu.

She came back after a few minutes and took my order. Afterwards, she lingered, wanting to make conversation, and asked me if it was my first time visiting.

'No, not really,' I replied. 'But it is a very long time since I was here.'

'And has it changed much?' she asked.

'Maybe. I don't know,' I said, shaking my head. 'It seems so familiar, but it's also different.' I paused. 'Do you know what happened to Lucas Hope?'

'Lucas Hope?'

I nodded.

She considered and then shook her head. 'I don't know the name. Who is he?'

'He used to run this pub. A long time ago now, I guess.'

'No, I don't know. Adam runs it now with his wife. He's had it for five years or so. I don't know about before that.'

'Has it always been called The Black Dog? I remembered it as being something else.'

'What was it?"

'The Green Man, I think. I remember the sign.'

'There's a Green Man at Blackthorpe. Perhaps you're thinking of that one?'

I shook my head.

'No, here. For sure.'

She shrugged and moved off to serve another customer. I drank my wine and pondered.

'Do you know who lives in Walnut Cottage?' I asked, when she was free again.

'Walnut?'

'Yes, a little house, halfway up the road to the church on the left, set back from the road. Perhaps it's not called that any more. I knew someone who lived there once upon a time.'

'No, I don't know the name. But there is an empty place for sale or rent up there, I think. There's a sign.'

People came and went. To my great relief I didn't recognise any of them. I drank two glasses of wine and ate a dressed crab – the local speciality – and a bowl of chips. I felt I was inside a dream. I had good reason to believe that was actually the case.

Later, I walked up the familiar road. They say that the past is a foreign country but this was not quite like that. The present was a foreign country and the past was home. Yet there were subtle changes: misregistrations of memory, slippages. A tree I remembered bulged and twisted in a way I had not noticed before, a front door was blue and not white, there were wallflowers instead of daisies in the verges before the cottages. A

179

telegraph pole here in the wrong place. At our gate I hesitated. The gate – old, sagging, green with moss and mould – was shut. A number had been crudely painted on it in white paint, now faded and obscure. A timber had been nailed to the fence post and to it was attached a gaudy 'For Rent' sign. I recognised the name of the agency. Had I been at school with a boy of that name? I looked up and down the lane. There was no one to be seen and I laid my hand on the gate to push it open, half expecting to feel some sort of psychic vibration, a tremor passing through the fabric of reality, or an echo welling up from the distant past. But there was nothing. Still I hesitated. I was not quite ready. I carried on walking up the hill, thinking to see the church and the view across the marshes, to orientate myself in this landscape which was at once so familiar and so alien, before taking the crucial next step.

I reached the church quickly. Looking out across the wide landscape it was as if I were airborne again. Airy. That old feeling. The light was bright and the air was clear, just as it was when I recalled that place and that view out to the ocean. An extraordinary luminescence hung over the sea and the marshes and I recalled Mother telling me about a particular optical effect that occurred when reflected light mingled with direct light, so that objects in the field of vision had their own internal radiance, and space itself appeared to glow, a nothingness lit from within.

I laid a hand on the cold flint of the church walls. Cold glass. Opaline. Celestial. Closely knapped. I had never before noticed or paid attention to the extraordinary skill and precision of that stonework. Each stone was in exactly the right place. My old bench was still there and I sat on it and passed into what I can only describe as a sort of trance, intoxicated with the light and space and above all the freighted silence, once upon a time so known and yet now so unnerving after many years of urban living. This was not what I had expected or hoped for. But equally, what exactly I had expected and hoped for I could not possibly say.

As I sat by the church, as I had done so many times in my past life, I was seized by a kind of paralysis, to the extent that I wondered if I would even be able to set foot in our yard and then make my cautious way into the back garden. In my mind's eye it was tangled and unruly, untended and overgrown, run wild, brambled, and where (I assumed) the tree was waiting for me, still, impassive, patient. Or – and this might be even more terrible – I could find a neatly manicured green lawn, polite and ordered flowerbeds, a tidy and busy vegetable patch, and no tree at all.

Some time passed, my heartbeat subsided and the tingling sensation left me, and I roused myself. I walked around the church, recognising the inscriptions on the headstones, and then went inside to see the Mermaid.

The third pew back on the left-hand side has a carved end panel. Set in a kind of frame, she looks out, confidently. The Mermaid's long hair streams behind and around her, reaching down to her waist and merging with the swirling sea, becoming just an extension of it. Her tail is coiled around, forming a tight spiral. In one hand she holds a goblet and in the other, a key. She is well known, an esoteric curiosity, and some people even travel to the village specifically to see her.

The story was that, at one time, when the church was still filled every Sunday with the people of the village and also the surrounding lands, a beautiful lady began to attend the services. No one knew her and she had never been seen before in those parts. She came every week and was a fine singer. Her voice bewitched all the men in the congregation but none so much as Adam Goodman, a fisherman who also sang in the choir. It was said that their two voices entwined in harmony could melt any heart. The services at the church were filled with music lovers who had heard of the wondrous singing and who came just to hear it.

One Sunday neither the lady nor Adam Goodman appeared. The next day Adam Goodman's empty boat was seen to be moored at the quay when the other fishermen went out. The day after that was the same. In fact, Adam Goodman was seen no more and the lady never came to the church again. But soon after, people reported hearing singing out in the marshes, and the fishermen, especially at night, would hear singing out at sea. So people said that the lady had been a mermaid and their singing had been a kind of courtship, and she had compelled Adam Goodman to give up life on land and join her beneath the waves. They said they lived happily ever after, of course. That's how it sometimes goes in those stories.

I remembered the telling of the tale at school, and how after we had been tasked with drawing pictures to illustrate the story in coloured pencils. In my naive and fanciful rendering of their submarine dwelling I reached for vivid blues, greens and oranges. Discussing the story with Mother at home that evening, she had said that in fact the pew had been carved by a talented woodworker – she couldn't remember his name – who had lived in the village in the twenties. He had been commissioned to make a number of objects for the church over the years, including the lectern, candlesticks, stools and chairs. The myth of the mermaid had been invented afterwards to explain the presence of such an unusual object in a place of holy worship. There had never been a lady with a silken voice and there had never been anyone called Adam Goodman. It was just a story.

She smiled. *Not every story is true,* she said.

At the time I was profoundly disappointed by this revelation. I had enjoyed the fantasy of the mermaid and the fisherman, imagining their home beneath the sea, all shimmering emerald greens and lapis blues. Later I had come to enjoy the dissonance between truth and fiction. Something about the contrast between the telling of the story and the spell it had cast, the luminous and living images it summoned from the well of my imagination, and then the refutation – the revelation that it was but a fabricated enchantment – was profoundly satisfying to me. It seemed to me then – and still does – that in this lay a paradoxical truth.

The carved wood is polished and so dark with age as to be almost black. It looked like stone in the pale light that filtered in and filled the church. I left and began to retrace my steps down the hill. I was being drawn forward upon a length of thread, as if in the labyrinth, wound in and on. At the gate I hesitated again, but this time I pushed it open and passed through.

The front garden is approximately as I remember it, but ragged and overgrown. Someone has given the grass a rough cut in recent weeks, but it is already getting long again, rangy and yellowing in the sunlight.

The house is smaller than I remember, almost entirely encased in the thick glossy foliage of the creeper, as if trying to conceal itself from the world. I push the leaves aside and peer in through one of the front windows; into an empty space, dusty and shadowed. The carpet and the painting that used to hang on the wall above the fireplace, which I remember so well, are of course long gone, and the vacant room looks unbearably melancholy. My face is reflected ambiguously in the glass: a ghost in an empty chamber.

I pass around to the side of the house and try the handle on the door. It is locked. The paint on the door is cracked and peeling, revealing many layers: dark blue, pale yellow, grey, green, and a sky blue, which I think might be the one we had all those years ago. The corners of the porch are thick with dusty cobwebs holding the husks of small flying creatures and on a nail by the door there hangs a disintegrating corn dolly.

The garden is divided. The passage into the back is blocked by a fence overgrown with vigorous climbers: black bryony and bittersweet with its hanging bunches of poisonous egg-shaped berries. There is a gate and I undo the latch and peer through. It is not as I expected. Stepping through – pushing through – is like passing a portal, crossing a threshold into an alternate reality, into what almost feels like an *interior* space.

There is an insane profusion. Before me is a thick stand of henbane, unpleasant, somewhat ominous-looking, evil-smelling, about four feet tall, stout and hairy. Its sticky leaves are covered in down. Its large, tubular flowers are creamy brown with networks of purplish veins and are a ripe and meaty purple inside. I remember that Gramper called it Granny's Dream and once explained that it could be used as a sedative. At first it is all utterly unfamiliar, but quickly I get my bearings and can map the parameters of the garden as it was. To say that the garden is overgrown is a gross understatement. It is teeming. I am witness to a grotesque fecundity, a concentrated zone akin to lush rainforest or even jungle. I am confronted by a dense mass of green growth reaching up to the sky, articulated by an armature of branches, stretching from one side of the space to the other: overgrown, entangled; knotted and twisted. In the centre of it all is the tree. His form is unmistakeable. He is bigger than I remember, more complex, crowned with bright leaves, entwined with tendrils, trailers, vines, twisting and gripping. His limbs which were once so slender are now thick and knotted, muscled even, encased in hard craggy bark and almost quivering with potency. Sprays of flowers hang among the glossy, dark green leaves of King's Joy, draping his arms and shoulders. Underfoot, pale ferny fronds compete with tangled ground creepers. Everything is overripe. You can smell this ripeness, like everything has gone too far. The atmosphere is rich with a heady and intoxicating scent, the very air a narcotic miasma.

Mischiefs manifest.

A bizarre multitude of plants are aseasonally and illogically massed together in the space as if pushing closer to him: gipsywort, its bell-shaped flowers dotted with purple; agrimony; eyebright; black nightshade, with its peculiar greeny-black berries; greater stitchwort; broomrape; goldenrod. All are flowering, profusely and crazily. It is too much.

The whole scene is shot through with flashes of brilliant colour: flower bursts of vermilion, corn yellow, lilac, magenta. There are bright white blooms strung through the branches like luminous *faerie* lights.

The light shimmers. The spaces between things are golden and filled with dappled vibration. Shafts of light lance down between the branches and hold a myriad of dust motes like constellations, and insects – bees, lacewings, butterflies, craneflies, even a stately azure dragonfly like a venerable aviator – spiral around in an ecstatic aerial dance.

The air is thick, like honey.

I am struck with the sensation of warmth, as if heat is being generated somewhere nearby. I am struck also by a weird jubilance, as if this thronging vitality is rejoicing in its very existence.

I climb through the growth towards the back of the garden where there is a space that is more open, and I am filled with an extraordinary compulsion to lie down on the ground. Normally I would lie on my back, look up into the sky and enjoy the feeling of the cold weight of the earth behind me. But I lie face down, pushing aside leaves of enchanter's nightshade and fronds of skullcap in order to press my face against the teeming ground. It is cool down here at ground level. My nostrils fill with a different kind of scent, of earth, mulch, decay, disintegration: rich, meaty, organic. Mushrooms are below me in the darkness, tiny pockets of potential, waiting for the perfect moment to push upwards into quick life.

My left hand is stretched out and can just touch the base of a stout stem of thornapple, about three feet tall, exuding an unpleasant scent. It has glossy pointed oval leaves like holly and bears large purple and white trumpet flowers. Again, I remember Gramper's advice, that its seeds are narcotic and that cigarettes rolled from the leaves are said to alleviate the symptoms of asthma.

My right hand rests on a patch of coarse grass sprouting with common campions, with pink and burgundy flowers. Twisting my neck, I see high above me that the canopy of the higher trees growing at the edges of the garden encircles a small blue patch of sky, a hanging jewel, and is entwined with pungent hops and sweet-smelling dog rose. My cheek rests on bare soil and I stare straight into low-growing dog's mercury and deadly nightshade. There are rat's tails frosted with spider's webs and the whole low landscape is alive with busy ants and beetles, parading hither and thither in yet another complex dance.

Turning my head I glimpse the dark gemstone eye of a snake, watching me knowingly. An adder, a big one. But I am not afraid. Unusually, he is brick red instead of the usual greyish brown, with dark markings zigzagging along his back. He holds my gaze. With what looks like a nod, he turns smoothly and slides soundlessly away into the shadows.

I lie spread-eagled, extended. Power is pulsing through me, a great throbbing and humming. It fills me up and echoes around inside me as if I am a hollow chamber. I become a receptor.

I have the feeling that this garden recognises me. It welcomes me.

And now, here comes the old dream, or memory, or fantasy, or whatever it is, for the first time in what seems like many years. Pressed against the ground I begin to shift and change, my skin puckers and tiny tendrils emerge and begin to push downwards into the soft warm earth. At the same time roots and shoots from below break the surface and push up and through me. I am absorbed and absorbing, transfigured.

Time passes and I am lost in the shadows.

*

When I come back to consciousness the light has changed. I am surprised to see that several hours have passed by and the sun is dipping low. There is a hum of activity, of insects crawling and flying, buzzing from flower to flower, and birds are calling to one another somewhere above. I climb unsteadily to my feet, brushing leaves and dirt from my clothes.

It is time to go home, though I wonder where *home* really is.

However, before I leave I need to touch him. I step through the dense growth, pushing leaves and flowers away from my face, until I am in his orbit. I stretch out my hand, cautiously, as if expecting an electric shock or worse.

I touch him. The bark is hard and rough.

I leave the garden, pushing slowly back through the foliage and the little gate in the fence. Again, I have the sensation of crossing a threshold. On the other side, space and light open up and the air seems fresher and cleaner, unlike the heady narcotic atmosphere of the dense thicket that surrounds the tree.

I push through the gate into the lane. All is quiet. I need to walk, to set one foot in front of the other and breathe deeply, so as to order my thoughts. I set off up the lane, climbing up past the church and heading for the heath. It will take several hours but my intention is to walk across the heath and then through the woods and so back to the town, where I will stay the night.

At the top of the lane I pass the crossroads where once upon a time I would have turned left to take the way to Quill's house. There is a gate where the path sets out across the heath. Another tree that I remember well stands there. Once, one Sunday while still at primary school, Quill and I climbed up into its branches and found comfortable crooks to sit in, from where we could see people ascending the hill to the church for worship. We stayed up there for a very long time, enjoying the tree view, the change in perspective the vantage point offered. Eventually, we took out my penknife and carefully cut our initials – AA and QQ – into the bark. Now, I peer up and see if I can spot those letters, but can see nothing.

The heath is as it always was. I walk the trail, which I have not trodden for more than two decades. Even with my eyes closed I would know the way. The heath is as beautiful as ever. Wild and unruly stands of spiked gorse glow bright yellow in the pale light, and the path winds through copses of beech trees and areas dominated by thick bracken and scrubby bushes. The path is lined with bright red and white-spotted fly agaric. Into the woods there is cool and shade beneath the gnarly oaks and high pines. At one point I come across a tiny muntjac, almost too small and fragile to be believable, and we stand, each contemplating the other, for a long time before she skips off into the undergrowth. Cock pheasants swagger between the trees, stupid and brazen. Crows caw from the treetops.

When we were little, we used to scare ourselves silly by making up stories about something that lived in those woods. We would say, relishing the alliteration, *Griselda Grubb* will get you if you say her name while the moon is full. *Spinning Stephen* is waiting. *Vinegar Victor* will steal into your room and gobble you up if you don't say your prayers. *Faceless Frank* will take your skin for a lamp shade. But the one that haunted me was the Wood Meg. *Don't go into the woods after dark, for the Wood Meg will carry you off. She'll use your bones and teeth and hair for making spells.*

The first time I heard the story, Bill Castle, Quill and I were debating the question of ghosts. Bill believed firmly that they did exist. I was undecided. But Quill had a surprisingly complex take on the question.

'There *are* ghosts,' she said. 'But not out there. They come from inside us. It's not like they are out there waiting for someone to come along. No, they're inside us. You know, like memories or dreams or something.'

'Like a projection?' I asked.

'Well, yes, I suppose that's one way to explain it. But I mean more like the way you can see things – people and places – when you close your eyes. You know, you *visualise* them. And, well, certain places can trigger those visualisations and then we think we see them, but they're not *really* there. Do you see what I mean? They're in our mind's eye.'

We nodded our heads.

'But how does that explain what happens when two people see the same thing, the same ghost?' I asked.

'It's the place,' she said. 'Like being tuned into a radio.'

We sat in silence for a bit, trying to wrap our thoughts around Quill's theory.

'Have you ever seen one?' asked Bill.

We shook our heads.

'I have,' he said, grinning. 'In the woods.'

We laughed, disbelieving.

'I have, I swear it! It was night. I saw the Wood Meg.'

The Wood Meg. I had not heard that strange name before.

190

'What did it look like?' asked Quill.

'Like black mist. But alive, somehow.'

I laughed again. 'If it was night and she looked like black mist, how did you see her? And what were you doing up in the woods at night anyway?'

We didn't believe him for a moment and ribbed him about it until he could take no more.

Bill sulked after that. But I remember that mentions of something malefic in the woods kept coming up in conversation from then on and began to have a cumulative effect. You know how it is when you become aware of something for the first time, and then you see it everywhere. It was like that. Griselda Grubb. Gwen Witch. King Leaf. It began to gnaw at me, the idea that there *was* something in the woods.

I asked Gramper about it, and he didn't exactly reassure me. 'Well,' he said, 'the world is very strange indeed, as you yourself know, and there are undoubtedly many things we don't understand. There are old things too, that have been around a whole lot longer than us, and we'll only see them when we're ready to see them.'

Whatever it was, it walked in the old woods at the edge of the heath. By day it was an old oak tree, but by night a malevolent shape-shifting presence that preyed on children. Was it a local legend or did we just make it up? I think the latter. I don't remember any adult ever mentioning it, and I don't remember ever asking my parents about it, only Gramper. I think it was just the product of our overheated little minds, perhaps inspired by the shapes of trees in the dusk: the grasping claw, the hunched crow, the jawless skull, the dog's head, the broken wing; all those suggestive silhouettes against the fading sky.

I visualised it so intensely – in the woods, stealing across the marsh, hiding behind hedges, creeping up the stairs – that for years I had nightmares in which I walked a path into the woods, the darkness gathering about me, the moon high in the sky above, shafts of zinc-pale light falling through the canopy. I come to a clearing and in the centre is a twisted and gnarly old oak, impossibly old. But as I look at it, something changes. The trunk shifts, going out of focus, and a figure – Griselda, Stephen, Meg, call it what you will – simply *steps out* of the tree and walks towards me. I don't see the face, just smoke and shadows where it should be, but as it advances the figure becomes taller, swiftly growing until it towers above me. Invariably, I would then wake, twisting the blankets in a panic, breathless, the forest shadows and the scent of leaf mould fading.

I walk inland and it is almost dark when I arrive back at the little town at the end of the railway line, from where I had started my walk that morning. On the market square is a pub where they have a room for me. In the room I wash and lie down on the bed and close my eyes. The events of the day unspool like the film of a fever dream.

I am unable to rest; my thoughts and memories are churning like a sea in a storm. I go down to the bar.

As I order a drink the barman asks, 'Good day?' and I'm uncertain how to respond. Has it been a good day? I'm really unsure what kind of day it has been. I nod and attempt a smile. He doesn't linger, thankfully.

I take a simple supper in a quiet corner. The fear of being

recognised returns and I deliberately choose a table quite hidden, but from where I can have a view of the bar. Luckily, it is quiet and I need make no conversation.

I work my way through a bottle of wine, trying to wash away something indefinable. I drink slowly as my thoughts spiral around. I have a nagging sense of a journey not finished, of a text not fully read; of something waiting just beyond the edge of my consciousness. This visitation of the past has reawakened the presence of this landscape and reminded me again of its importance to me. I am part of it and it is part of me. That seems obvious now. It had always been there but now it is alive again. I am thinking about Prospero and Ariel and Caliban, and enchantment and trickery, and Mother and Father and Gramper. The waves wash gently against the shingle banks as the light fades and the reeds and grasses of the marsh sway in the wind. The tide is coming in and dark water pours into the dikes and cuts, where birds and beasts are settling for the night. An owl calls in the wood and is answered.

Griselda Grubb is walking. The Wood Meg flits from shadow to shadow. The deer stir, unsettled.

As I sit there, sipping at my glass of red wine, a thought comes to me. So strange that I must turn it over in my mind, like a pebble found upon the beach and placed in a pocket and then forgotten, only to be discovered anew at some later date.

Finally, I am able to go up. Before I get into bed, I pull aside the curtains and look out of the open window, across the Market Square with its war memorial, across the roofs of the town. Beyond lies the wood and the heath, and then the marshes and the sea. Beyond that is infinity. The air is cool and the moon and stars are bright in the sky. Everything glows from within; irradiated.

I sleep almost immediately and there are no dreams.

In the morning I rise early. To get home I will not retrace my steps but will catch a bus back inland to the city, and from there the train south. But first I wander through the small town. Some of the shops are familiar but most have changed. It has been a long time.

In one of the streets off the square I recognise the estate agent's sign and go in. A man of about my age, who seems vaguely familiar, rises to greet me and ask if he might help. He wears a suit and tie. His round face is ruddy red and friendly. I ask for the details of the cottage.

'No one has asked about that one for quite a while,' he says.

'I'm not surprised,' I say. 'I was there yesterday and it's in quite a state. I didn't go in, obviously, but I could see that the garden in particular is very overgrown.'

He nods.

'I probably shouldn't say this, but there is a rumour that it's, well, not exactly haunted, but that there is something unusual about it.' He says this carefully. 'There was an incident there a few years ago.'

'An incident?'

'Yes, a child went missing. Never found. Very sad. Probably out on the marshes.'

I nod and he grins, embarrassed.

'It's always been a hard one to place. No one has taken it in quite a while. It's why the rent is so good.'

'Nonetheless, it's in a nice position,' I say.

'That's very true. It's a pleasant village and the sea is right there on the doorstep. Some of the best birding in the country, if that's your thing.'

I nod and look carefully at the sheet of paper he hands me.

'How long might you want it for?' he asks.

Acknowledgements

Profound thanks are due.

To my agent, Charlotte Seymour, who made it happen. To everyone at Little, Brown, but especially to Rhiannon Smith, for belief and for seeing a way to make the book a better one; to Amy Perkins for sensitive editing; to Nithya Rae for guiding *The North Shore* into being; to David Bamford and Steve Gove for their careful copy editing and proofreading respectively; and to Hannah Wood for the beautiful cover.

To the early readers; Rebecca Goss, for feedback and valuable advice; and to Julian Marshall, for friendship and encouragement.

To the fellow travellers – Emile Cassen, Sandy Foster, Billy Green, Catherine Johnstone, Conor McAnally, Niamh McAnally, Lisa Orban, Nina Smith and Wendy Williams – for support and positive thinking.

To The Aleph, who first published the episode with the whale in my limited-edition chapbook, *Dissolution*.

To my parents, Ron and Sue, who moved us to Norfolk in 1976 but never got to see the strange book that the land dreamt in me.

To Pablo and Tomás, and to Cecilia, for everything.